Lara Lacombe earned [...] immunology and worke[d] [...] country before moving into the classroom. Her day job as a college science professor gives her time to pursue her other love—writing fast-paced romantic suspense with smart, nerdy heroines and dangerously attractive heroes. She loves to hear from readers! Find her on the web or contact her at laralacombewriter@gmail.com.

Also by Lara Lacombe

Discover more at millsandboon.co.uk

COLTON K-9 BODYGUARD

LARA LACOMBE

MILLS & BOON

First Published in Great Britain 2018
by Mills & Boon, an imprint of HarperCollins*Publishers*
1 London Bridge Street, London, SE1 9GF

Colton K-9 Bodyguard © 2018 Harlequin Books S.A.

ISBN: 978-0-263-26564-4

39-0318

MIX
Paper from
responsible sources
FSC™ C007454

This one is for Mae.

Chapter 1

"Are you sure you really want to do this?"

Beatrix Colton's heart sank as Jennifer Sheridan nodded.

"I have to," the young woman said sadly. She gave the poufy white dress one last, longing look before pushing it across the counter. Bea grabbed the hanger and hung the dress on the hook next to the register, smoothing out the full skirt with the palm of her hand.

Now came the awkward part. "I'm afraid I can't offer you a refund, since you've already had your final fitting," she said delicately.

"I know." Jennifer blinked back tears and shook her head. "I hate this," she said, sniffing. "But Mark and I have talked about it, and I just can't risk his safety."

"I understand," Bea assured her. And, truthfully, she did. "The Groom Killer has us all scared. I don't blame you for wanting to be careful, especially right now."

"Mark said I'm overreacting," Jennifer confessed. She looked down, then met Bea's eyes. "But I think he's secretly relieved we're canceling the wedding. One less thing to worry about, you know?"

Bea nodded sympathetically.

"We're being very public about the cancellation. That's why I'm here—everyone has to see me return this dress."

"Of course," Bea murmured.

"I had hoped the police would have captured the killer by now," Jennifer continued. She eyed Bea speculatively, and Bea realized the woman was waiting for her to chime in with a juicy detail about the investigation. Everybody in town thought Bea's cousin, Demi Colton, was the Groom Killer who'd murdered two men the night before their weddings—one in January, and one last month in February. Bea herself wasn't so sure; she didn't know Demi all that well, but she hated to jump to conclusions about something so serious.

"I'm sure they'll find whoever is doing this soon," Bea replied, trying to sound noncommittal. She wasn't in the mood to discuss her cousin or any other topic related to the Groom Killer. She'd already lost a lot of business, thanks to panicked couples canceling their nuptials in the hopes of staying off the killer's radar. If the police didn't find the culprit soon, Bea's Bridal Salon would have to close.

It was a possibility that made her sick to her stomach.

Forcing a smile, Bea changed the subject. After a moment, Jennifer realized Bea wasn't going to reveal any family secrets, and she gathered up her purse to leave.

"I really am sorry about this," she said, pausing at the door.

Just go, Bea thought, practically willing the woman to leave.

"I understand," Bea repeated. "I hope you'll come back once your wedding is back on."

"Oh, I will," Jennifer promised.

Bea nodded, but the woman's reassurance didn't make her feel any better. The possibility of future business was nice, but it wouldn't help her pay the bills now.

And that was the problem.

Since Bea's Bridal Salon didn't exactly offer a diverse array of services, there wasn't much she could do to draw in clients while the shadow of the Groom Killer lingered over them all.

Her father, Fenwick Colton, had offered to float her some funds until things returned to normal. But Bea refused to use his money. This was *her* shop, and she wasn't going to take charity from anyone.

Especially not dear old Dad.

Bea had inherited the bridal shop after her grandmother's death five years ago. She'd seen it as both a gift and an opportunity; Bea had spent countless hours in the shop as a child, falling under the spell of the beautiful dresses and the happy brides. She'd spent many an afternoon walking among the gowns, daydreaming about her own wedding. There was something magical about a wedding dress, and she loved seeing the look on a woman's face when she found her perfect one. It was an experience that never got old, and it was the reason Bea loved her job.

But her father and siblings hadn't seen it that way. Fenwick had viewed the shop as a burden, something to be sold quickly so he wouldn't have to deal with it. When Bea had embraced the chance to own the boutique, her father had been shocked and disappointed. He'd argued long and hard against it, telling her it was beneath her dignity as a Colton to do such work. He thought Bea should marry a rich man and spend her time lunching and volunteering, as all well-bred women did. When Bea refused to fall in line, Fenwick threatened to use his position as Red Ridge's mayor to make sure the shop failed. But Bea had held firm, and eventually her father had accepted the fact that he wasn't going to be able to change her mind.

The grandfather clock began to chime the hour, drawing Bea out of her thoughts. The familiar sound was comforting, and for a moment, she could almost feel her grandmother's presence, as if the kind woman's spirit had come for a visit.

"Don't worry, Gram," Bea said quietly. "I'll find a way to make this work."

She walked over to the front door of the shop and

flipped the Open sign to Closed. She drew the shades down on the windows and returned to the register. It wouldn't take long to close up tonight—no one had bought a dress in days.

Jennifer's returned gown caught her eye as she moved to the back room. The orphaned dress had a forlorn look about it now, as if the bride's rejection had soaked into the fabric.

Bea shook her head at the fanciful thought and grabbed the dress off the hook. She'd need to inspect it carefully for signs of damage, but it appeared to be in perfect condition. Maybe Jennifer really would come back for it, once the Groom Killer had been caught. If not, perhaps Bea could sell it to another bride...

There was a muffled thump from the direction of the stockroom, and Bea paused in her journey to the back office. She was the only one in the store, so what had caused the noise? Her thoughts flashed to the bakery a few doors down. A pregnant stray cat had gotten in there once, looking for a warm place to deliver. The mama cat and kittens had all been adopted. Maybe another mama cat was looking for shelter from South Dakota in March.

Placing the dress on a nearby rack, Bea headed for the stockroom. She hadn't gone more than a few steps when the lights flickered off, plunging the store into darkness.

The fine hairs on her arms lifted and she froze, her breath catching in her throat.

"Hello?" she called out uncertainly. She shook her

head, feeling foolish. She was the only one in the store, and the lights had probably gone out thanks to a power surge. All she needed to do was walk over to the circuit box and flip the breaker switch back into position. Simple enough, right?

"Right," she whispered to herself. Bea resumed her walk toward the stockroom, but she couldn't shake the feeling that something was not quite right...

She heard a rustling from the front of the store. Was someone coming to rob her?

Lights, she thought, panic rising up her throat. *Turn on the lights.* If the store really was being robbed, the illumination might spook the would-be thief. She wasn't brave enough to stick around, though—as soon as she flipped the breaker switch, she was going to escape out the back. Just as she stepped through the door, she caught a whiff of perfume. It was so unexpected, Bea drew up short, confused. She didn't wear perfume, and she didn't use air fresheners in the store to prevent the dresses from absorbing odors. Where had the smell come from? And why was it familiar? There was something about the scent that tickled her memory, but before she could put her finger on it, Bea heard a noise to her right. She turned, straining to make out a shape in the darkness. Air blew past her face as someone moved, and then her world exploded in a starburst of pain.

"Well, what do you think?"

Officer Micah Shaw shrugged at the question. "I think we're out here on a wild goose chase. You?"

Officer Brayden Colton nodded. "Yeah. It's starting to look that way to me, too." He sighed. "I don't know whether to be relieved, or…" He trailed off, and Micah filled in the blanks.

"You still think Demi is innocent."

"She's my sister," Brayden said simply. "The Demi Colton I know is not a cold-blooded killer."

Micah didn't respond. There wasn't anything he could say, really. Brayden had grown up with Demi and they were family, so naturally he didn't want to believe she was the Groom Killer. But the evidence suggested otherwise. Most of the Coltons on the Red Ridge police force had a hard time believing one of their own could turn to murder, and Brayden in particular thought his sister was being framed. Micah wasn't as idealistic. As a former Army Ranger who'd served in Afghanistan, he'd seen the worst of humanity. Nothing shocked him anymore.

"You want to take the far end, and we'll search down here?" he suggested.

Brayden nodded. "That works. We'll at least be able to say we covered the whole area when we go back to the office."

The two men parted ways, and Micah and his K-9 partner, Chunk, set off down the darkening alley.

Personally, he thought they were wasting their time. Chunk was the best cadaver dog in the state— hell, the region—and he'd been placid and calm ever since they'd set foot in the alley. A far cry from the behavior Micah would expect if there was a body present. But since Tucker Frane had stumbled into the station earlier, claiming he saw Demi Colton shoot a man in this very alley just a little while ago, the police had to respond.

Micah, Chunk and Brayden had been dispatched to search the area. So far, all they'd found were a few discarded coffee cups and some cigarette butts. Not exactly the stuff of a crime scene. But they had a job to do, and Micah bagged it all. He was nothing if not thorough…

"Come on, boy," he said encouragingly to Chunk. "Let's see if there's anything to find."

Chunk waddled alongside Micah, the tips of his ears dragging along the ground as he moved. The red and white basset hound was never going to win any beauty contests, but he had one of the best noses Micah had ever seen.

This wasn't Micah's first time working with a furry partner. He'd been paired with a military working dog while serving as an Army Ranger, and the experience had made him appreciate and respect the capabilities of these hardworking animals. Chunk was unlike any dog he'd known, and it had taken some time for Micah to get used to his quirks. But now that they knew each other, he wouldn't trade Chunk for any other dog in the world.

They wandered slowly down the alley, Micah automatically adjusting his stride to accommodate Chunk's shorter legs. Chunk kept his nose pressed to the ground, snuffling as he walked, taking in all the scents and likely filing them away for later. Micah knew the dog's nose could detect thousands, if not tens of thousands, of smells, and it still amazed him that Chunk could sort through all the olfactory "noise" and zero in on the scent of human blood.

He was content to walk alongside Chunk, letting the dog move at his own pace. Even though he doubted they would find anything, this was a good exercise for Chunk. Micah began to let his mind wander, wondering who, exactly, Tucker Frane had seen tonight. The man had been almost frantic as he'd told them about the shooting he'd witnessed. He'd kept looking over his shoulder, as if he expected Demi Colton to stride into the station and shoot him in front of a squad of police officers. Finn Colton, the K-9 unit chief, had wanted Tucker to stick around and answer more questions, but the man had refused. He'd lit out of there like his pants were on fire.

"Let him go," Finn had said dryly. "I'll send some men out to talk to him later. In the meantime…"

Why would the man lie? Micah wondered. His story was easily verifiable. What did Tucker stand to gain by sending the police on a fool's errand?

Chunk suddenly pulled against his lead, interrupting Micah's thoughts. He focused on the dog, who was now staring intently at the door of one of the stores. "Find something?" Micah asked softly.

Chunk made a low *ruff* sound in response, and Micah felt his heart pick up speed. He gave the dog his head, and Chunk led him directly to the door, which Micah could now see was ajar. He realized with a little shock that it was the back door to Bea Colton's bridal salon, and his gut tightened. He hadn't seen Bea since he'd left for basic training. Once upon a time, he'd thought she was the love of his life. He'd learned the truth the hard way, and the lesson still stung.

Chunk huffed at the door and Micah carefully pulled it open. It was pitch-black inside the store, and he paused on the threshold. Chunk was trained to detect human blood, but he didn't have any way of communicating if he was scenting something fresh or old. If there was a body inside, Micah didn't want to surprise the killer and wind up with a bullet for his trouble.

"Police," he called out loudly. "Identify yourself."

He could hear the faint wail of a siren in the distance, but there was no sound from within the store. Moving carefully, Micah dropped Chunk's leash and grabbed his flashlight, keeping his other hand on the butt of his gun.

Chunk darted into the store, presumably heading for the source of the scent. Micah quickly swept the room with his flashlight, searching for any signs that he wasn't alone. The beam of light revealed nothing but racks of dresses and boxes stacked neatly on shelves. He took a breath and slowly exhaled, focusing on the feel of the room. He didn't sense anyone else, didn't hear any breathing or furtive sounds like someone was trying to hide. The place was empty.

There was a switch by the door, but it didn't work. He ran the beam of his light along the wall again until he caught the glint of the fuse box on the far side. He flipped a few breakers back into position, and the room flooded with light.

Micah blinked against the sudden brightness. "Chunk?" he called. He wasn't worried about the dog—Chunk would go to the source of the smell he'd detected and no farther.

Chunk barked once, and Micah oriented to the sound. He rounded a rack of dresses and found his partner sitting next to a body on the floor.

A very *feminine* body…

Micah knelt next to the dog, his breath caught in his throat. No. It couldn't be.

"Please, no," he whispered.

As the first on the scene, he had to help her. His hands shook a little as he reached out and grabbed the woman's shoulders. Carefully, slowly, he turned her onto her back and got a good look at her face.

The bottom dropped out of his stomach. It was Bea Colton.

Chapter 2

Micah stared down at Bea's bloody face, his heart in his throat. Was she—?

Her chest rose and fell, and relief washed over him as he realized she was still alive.

He reached for his walkie-talkie. "Brayden, I need backup. Call an ambulance." He quickly relayed his position and returned his focus to Bea. Chunk nosed him inquisitively, and he realized he had forgotten to reward the dog for his find.

"Good job, buddy." He dug in the pouch on his belt for a treat and absently handed it over. Chunk gobbled it up in one bite, then set about exploring the rest of the room.

"Bea?" Micah gently brushed the hair back from her forehead, noticing the nasty gash along her hairline as he did so. He glanced around, searching for something he could use to stanch the flow of blood from the wound. But all he saw were racks of wedding gowns and frilly lace veils. Bea would kill him if he ruined one of them, so he yanked his shirt from his belt and used his utility knife to cut off a strip from the T-shirt he wore underneath his button-down. It wasn't sterile, but it was the best he could do at the moment.

She didn't stir as he pressed the fabric to her head, and his worry grew. He wasn't sure how long she'd been unconscious, but since her wound was still bleeding freely, the attack was probably recent. But where was her assailant?

No one had run out of the store into the alley, at least not since he and Brayden had arrived. They must have escaped through the front door. For a split second, Micah considered checking to see if the door was unlocked, but he didn't want to leave Bea alone while she was still unconscious. Brayden would be here any minute, and he could look around for clues.

"Police!" Brayden's voice boomed into the otherwise silent store, and some of Micah's worry eased.

"Over here," he called.

Brayden was at his side in an instant, his gaze taking in the scene. "What happened?" He knelt beside Micah, frowning at the sight of Bea's bloody face. This was Brayden's cousin, and though Micah knew Bea's and Brayden's branches of the family weren't exactly close, it couldn't be easy to see her this way.

"Not sure," Micah replied. "Chunk alerted, and

when we came in, he found her. No signs of an intruder, but I'm thinking they escaped out the front door since we didn't see anyone in the alley."

"I'll go check." Brayden stood and headed for the stockroom door. "Uh, Micah?"

"What?"

"I think Chunk has found something else."

Micah turned to see the dog pacing back and forth in front of the door that led into the store proper. Chunk let out a low whine, and it was clear he was interested in something beyond the door.

"Can you take him?" he asked Brayden. "I don't want to leave her alone."

"No problem," Brayden replied. Technically, Chunk was trained to work with Micah, but he would be fine with Brayden for a moment, especially in a closed environment like the boutique. "Chunk," Micah commanded. "Go find."

The dog let out a happy yip and shot into the other room when Brayden opened the door. After a few seconds, Micah heard his characteristic alert bark and knew the dog had discovered something.

Another injured person? Or a corpse?

Micah kept his shirt pressed to Bea's head, silently willing her to wake up. He was no doctor, but the longer she stayed unconscious, the more his worry grew. "Come on, Bea," he said softly. "Wake up for me."

She stirred and her eyes fluttered open.

"Bea." He breathed out her name on a sigh of relief. "You're okay. I'm here."

Her dazed eyes focused on him. "Micah?" Her voice was weak, and her tone held a note of wonder as if she couldn't believe she was really seeing him.

"Yes, it's me. I'll take care of you."

"Don't leave me."

Her request pierced his heart. As if he could walk away from her now. "I won't. I'll stay with you. I promise."

She smiled faintly, then closed her eyes again and appeared to drift back into unconsciousness.

"Oh, no you don't. Wake up. Please keep talking to me."

She frowned slightly. "Hurts."

"I know, baby, but you need to stay awake."

"Okay," she said agreeably. But her eyes remained closed.

Where's the ambulance? he thought desperately. The sooner Bea got to the hospital, the better.

Brayden returned at that moment, Chunk by his side. The dog trotted over to Micah and nosed the pouch on his belt, clearly ready for another reward. "Well?" Micah asked as he gave Chunk a treat. He glanced at the pair and then returned his gaze to Bea. *Stay awake*, he silently pleaded with her.

Brayden crouched down and ran a hand through his hair. "The front door was open. Probably how her assailant got away."

Micah nodded. "And what else? What did Chunk find?"

His friend blew out a breath and a flash of misery

passed across his features. "There's a body in one of the fitting rooms. Looks like another victim of the Groom Killer."

Her head felt like it was going to split open.

Bea winced against the bright lights of the hospital room and tried to shield her face from the glare. But it was no use. Even with her eyes closed, she felt like she was being stabbed directly in the brain with a needle.

Suddenly, the room went dark. "Is that better?"

She turned to the sound of the deep voice she recognized even after all these years apart. Micah.

"Much. Thank you."

She cautiously opened her eyes to see the room was now in shadows. He'd flipped off the overhead lights and turned on the small bulb mounted under the wall cabinet. Her doctors probably wouldn't appreciate working in the gloom, but it helped downgrade her headache from excruciating to manageable, and for that she was grateful.

Micah settled into a chair by her bed. "You stayed," she said, a little surprised to still see him.

He met her eyes, his green gaze steady. "I promised I would."

"Yes, but..." She trailed off. They had made promises to each other before, promises that hadn't been kept.

Bea took a moment to study his face. It was still familiar, of course. But he'd changed in the years they'd been apart. Micah had always had a boyish glint in his eyes, a gleam of humor that persisted no matter how serious the situation. She was sad to see it was gone now, and wondered if it was hidden, or if his experiences in the war had permanently changed his personality. There were subtle lines around his mouth and eyes, a testament to the fact that he still smiled, at least. His skin was a warm gold, the product of time spent in the sun, no doubt. And he still had the same build, although he was a bit leaner, a bit harder now than when she'd known him in high school.

"You look good," she said quietly. There were so many things she wanted to say, and the questions piled up in her throat. *Why didn't you contact me after you left for basic training? Why didn't you respond to my letters and calls? Did you ever really love me?* But she swallowed the impulse to interrogate him. Did it really matter after all this time? It wasn't as if they could pick up where they'd left off. They had both been eighteen and supposedly in love. So much had happened since then, they were like two different people now. Two strangers, meeting for the first time.

A grin flashed across his face, there and gone in the space of a second. "I wish I could say the same for you," he said, his gaze darting meaningfully to the bandage on her head. His eyes softened. "This wasn't how I pictured meeting you again."

So he'd thought about her, after all? His words gave her a little thrill, but she quickly crushed the feeling. It was only natural she'd cross his mind. Red Ridge wasn't a huge city, and he'd probably figured it was only a matter of time until they ran into each other. She'd known he moved back to town after retiring from the military. But Bea had assumed she'd have time to mentally and emotionally prepare herself for seeing him again. Being confronted with his presence now brought up all kinds of emotions and feelings she had thought she'd conquered long ago. The experience was almost as unsettling as being attacked in her boutique.

A sudden commotion sounded from the hall, and she thought she heard the muffled boom of her father's voice. "Oh, no," she muttered.

Micah rose and headed toward the door. "I'll take care of it," he said confidently. "You just rest."

He was gone before she had a chance to thank him, leaving her alone in the dim room. She leaned her head back against the stiff pillow with a sigh, not knowing whether to be grateful or concerned that Micah had headed out to deal with her father. Fenwick Colton was hard-headed and stubborn and used to getting his way. And he and Micah had always been like oil and water, the two of them never seeing eye to eye. If her father was upset now, and it certainly sounded like he was, seeing Micah would likely send him over the edge.

But Bea was too tired to care right now. Micah wasn't the same boy she'd dated in high school, and it wouldn't take long for her father to realize that. Maybe Fenwick would view Micah as an adult now, and treat him accordingly instead of talking down to him like he always had.

"And maybe I'll sprout wings and fly out of here,"

she snorted. The chances of Micah and her father turning over a new leaf were next to impossible, but a girl could dream.

But…did it really matter? After all, she and Micah weren't exactly going to pick things up where they'd left off. She couldn't deny the idea was appealing. Part of her had never stopped loving Micah, and she wasn't going to lie to herself and pretend otherwise. That didn't mean he felt the same way about her, and even if he did, she wasn't sure she could forgive him for abandoning her all those years ago.

She shifted on the bed, the memories coming fast and furious now. Their last night together before Micah had left for basic training… They'd held each other all night, planning their future, picturing the life they would build together.

It'll be over before you know it, he'd whispered into her hair. *And once I'm done with basic training, I'll come back and we'll get married. I can't wait to see you wear my ring.*

She'd pressed her ear to his chest, loving the sound of his heartbeat in her ear. *I'll write to you every day*, she'd promised. *And I'll start planning the wedding.*

He'd left early the next morning, and she'd spent the rest of the week trying not to cry. True to her word, she'd written to him every day, sealing each letter with a kiss. She'd known he'd be too busy to write back, so it was an exciting surprise to find a letter from him about ten weeks after he left.

She'd raced up the stairs to her room, her heart pounding a mile a minute. Micah must be writing to tell her about when he was coming home, and to ask about the wedding plans. She'd been working hard to plan the ceremony—she wanted to keep things simple, which was almost unheard of her in family. But her father had made it clear he didn't approve of her relationship with Micah, and she wasn't about to ask him to pay for anything.

She'd flung herself onto the bed and carefully peeled open the envelope, withdrawing the letter. She'd felt a slight pang as she saw it wasn't very long—after so long apart, she wanted to know every detail of what he'd been up to—but she'd reminded herself he didn't have a lot of free time, and his sleep was more important that the length of his letters. She sank back onto a pillow, intending to savor every word. But as she started to read, her elation had quickly turned to confusion.

Dear Bea,
I'm sorry to end things like this, but I don't think we should be together anymore. Being away from you has made me realize we want different things, and I've come to realize that I can't be both a soldier and a husband. I don't need a wife tying me down and holding me back. I know this comes as a surprise, but I'm sure you'll find someone else.
Micah

Even after all these years, she could close her eyes and see the letter clear as day. The image was burned into her brain, each word chipping away at her heart until she felt like there was nothing left.

At first, she'd gone numb. After a few days, the pain had hit, followed quickly by anger. She'd written him back, demanding an explanation, needing to know why he'd changed his mind. She'd even tried calling, but that hadn't worked. Eventually, she'd worked her way into acceptance and decided to move on with her life.

That didn't stop her from checking the news on a daily basis, her worry spiking every time she heard about an American death. She scoured the internet, searching for the identities of fallen soldiers, breathing a little sigh of relief each time she realized Micah's name was not among the list of heroes.

She had tried to find love again, but it just never seemed to be in the cards. She'd dated a few men who were perfectly nice, but they never made her heart race and her skin tingle the way Micah had. Just being around him had been enough to make every nerve ending in her body stand up and pay attention. He had made her feel alive, made the world seem ripe with potential, as if anything and everything could happen at any moment.

It was so different from life in her father's house, where everything was carefully planned and executed, leaving no room for chance. Routine and structure were the guiding principles of her childhood, and she'd long ago realized she wanted—no, *needed*—more freedom. The men she'd dated since Micah had been safe, and had met with her father's approval. But marrying one of them would have guaranteed her future would echo her past, and she just couldn't bring herself to sign up for more of the same. Much to her father's chagrin, Bea had decided being single was preferable to a life spent yearning for more.

It hadn't been a difficult decision, and she hadn't had any doubts about her choice. Until now.

Could I be any more pathetic? She'd spent less than an hour in Micah's presence, and with a splitting headache to boot, and she was already questioning her hard-earned happiness. Logically, she knew she'd built a good life for herself and that she didn't need a man to find fulfillment or completion. *I'm doing just fine on my own*, she thought stubbornly.

But no matter how hard she tried, she couldn't ignore the persistent whisper of her heart.

He's the one.

Chapter 3

"I want to see my daughter. Right now." Fenwick Colton's voice rose in volume with every word until he was practically shouting in Micah's face. Micah took a deep breath and mentally counted to five. He'd never had the best relationship with Mr. Colton— the man had made it very clear he didn't approve of Micah dating Bea while they were in high school, and it seemed that time had not softened the sharper edges of the older man's temper.

"I'm sorry, but that's not possible at the moment," Micah said calmly. No matter how much he disliked Fenwick, he wasn't going to lose his control. If Micah showed any kind of emotion or anger, Fenwick would undoubtedly use it against him.

The man stepped forward, infringing on Micah's

personal space. "I know who you are," he hissed, staring up at Micah with obvious hatred in his eyes. "You're that skinny kid who tried to trap my Bea into marriage when she was just eighteen. Didn't you figure out she doesn't want you?"

The barb hit home, but Micah had expected a personal attack from Fenwick. He stared down at the man, his poker face in place. At this angle, Fenwick's blond toupee looked even more fake, and Micah realized that for all of Fenwick's bluster, he was likely very insecure.

"Is there a problem here?"

Both Micah and Fenwick turned at the sound of the voice, and Micah felt a jolt of relief as he caught sight of Finn Colton, the K-9 unit chief, approaching.

"No problem," Micah said smoothly. "I was just about to explain to Mister Colton the fact that Bea is a material witness in a murder case, and I don't want her speaking to anyone outside of her medical team until I've had a chance to interview her."

"You can't keep me from my daughter!" Fenwick shouted, his face growing red with anger.

Finn turned to his uncle.

"Actually, he can. Bea is an adult, and therefore you do not have a right to have access to her until the officer in charge of the investigation has completed his questioning."

Fenwick's expression grew murderous. "You're saying he's in charge of the investigation?" He jerked a thumb at Micah, evidently unwilling to even look at him anymore.

"That's correct," Finn confirmed. "As the officer who discovered both Bea and the victim in her shop, Micah is the man on point."

"But...but..." Fenwick sputtered. Then a sly look entered his eyes, and he shot Micah a satisfied glare before turning his attention back to Finn. "It's inappropriate for *Officer* Shaw to lead this investigation." He practically spat the word, making it clear just what he thought about Micah's job title. "He and my daughter have a history of personal involvement. I doubt he can be impartial about his job since Bea rejected him." He smiled triumphantly, clearly proud of himself.

Micah opened his mouth to explain that he hadn't seen Bea in years, but he needn't have bothered.

"That was ages ago," Finn said in a tone of long-suffering patience. "I have no doubts about Officer Shaw's capabilities, and I know he will conduct both himself and this investigation with the utmost professionalism."

Fenwick's smile slid off his face and his mouth turned down, giving him the look of a man who had just sucked on a lemon. "I see," he said, practically choking on the words. "Your superior officer will hear about this."

Finn nodded, as if he'd expected this reaction. "Let me know if you have trouble contacting him."

Fenwick walked to the far corner of the waiting room, his body stiff with anger. He was not used to being refused, and Micah could see that the older man did not handle disappointment very well.

"Thank you," Micah said in a low voice.

Finn nodded. "Anytime." He watched his uncle for a moment, then turned back to Micah. "Talk to me about what you found. Brayden wasn't too forthcoming about the details."

Micah related his actions in the alley and Chunk's discovery of Bea. "I called for backup, and once Brayden arrived he and Chunk went through the rest of the shop, searching for any signs of the intruder who had attacked Bea."

"So, Brayden made the initial discovery of the body in the fitting room?"

Micah nodded. "Yes. I went to the scene after the paramedics had arrived and were taking care of Bea."

"What did you find?"

"At first glance, another victim of the Groom Killer." Micah ran a hand through his hair. "Looked to me like Joey McBurn. He was slumped in a fitting room chair, and he appeared to have been shot through the heart. There was a black cummerbund stuffed into his mouth like the other two victims."

Finn digested this bit of information. "Any signs of tampering?" he asked delicately.

Micah frowned. "Not to my eye." Was the chief suggesting Brayden had altered the scene to throw suspicion off his sister, Demi? Micah supposed it was a possibility, but it hardly seemed likely. Everyone on the force knew Brayden Colton was upset at the thought of Demi as a killer, but he was still a good cop and an honorable man. Besides, any such tampering would be clearly evident once the forensics report came back, and Brayden knew that as well as the rest of the team.

But there was one other piece of information that made Micah confident his friend hadn't done anything stupid. "Brayden and Chunk weren't gone very long," he said. "And after they discovered the body, Brayden didn't return to the fitting room alone."

Finn nodded, apparently satisfied by this news. "That's good to know," he said. "It's important the investigation is above reproach."

"We're not going to drop the ball on this one," Micah said confidently.

"I know you won't," Finn replied. He angled his head in the direction of Bea's hospital room. "So, do you think she saw anything?"

"I'm not sure," Micah admitted. "It's possible the killer knocked her out before shooting Joey. Or maybe Bea heard the gunshot and went to explore, and that's when the killer attacked."

Finn frowned. "If that's the case, why is she still alive? Surely the perp wouldn't be so careless as to leave behind an eyewitness?"

"Maybe there wasn't time to kill her," Micah suggested. "It's possible the killer intended to finish her off, but got spooked and ran." *Or maybe*, he thought privately, *Demi couldn't stomach the thought of shooting her cousin.*

A cold chill skittered through his body at the thought of Bea lying unconscious on the ground, at the mercy of a murderer towering over her helpless body. Whatever the reason, Micah was glad Bea's life had been spared.

The elevator at the end of the hall let out a faint *ding*, and the doors opened to reveal Brayden along with Carson Gage, a fellow K-9 officer, and Shane Colton, a PI who worked with the department. The three men wore serious expressions, and Micah's interest spiked. What was going on?

Carson spoke first. "We've got news."

"Your initial witness, Tucker Frane, who claimed to see Demi Colton shoot someone in the alley?" said Shane. Micah nodded, and he continued. "Dead in his home."

"What?" That was too coincidental for Micah's taste.

Carson nodded. "Yep. We went to his house to ask him a few more questions about what he'd seen. He didn't answer, but the door was ajar so we entered. Man was shot dead in his recliner."

"No witnesses, I suppose?" Micah asked.

Shane shook his head. "Neighbors didn't see or hear anything."

"Of course not," Micah muttered. They rarely did.

"We put a rush on ballistics," Carson said. "We need to see if the same gun killed the witness and the man in the fitting room." He cast a subtle glance at Brayden.

"My sister didn't do this," Brayden said quietly. "I know she didn't."

"All we can go on is evidence," Finn said. "Her name written in blood by the body of the first victim. Her necklace found at the scene. She was spotted running in the shadows at the time of death. Now, we have a witness—a dead witness—who says he saw her shoot a man in the alley near Bea's shop."

"Two bodies in one night is strange," Carson put in.

"Two bodies?" The men turned as a group to find Fenwick Colton lurking on the edge of the circle, a cup of coffee in his hand. "Someone else was killed tonight?"

Micah clenched his jaw. He'd been so focused on listening to the other men he hadn't noticed Fenwick come back. Now the businessman was privy to information he shouldn't have, and Fenwick didn't know the meaning of the word discretion.

"Sir," he began, trying not to choke on the word.

Fenwick ignored him. "Why haven't you arrested Demi yet?" he demanded. "It's been clear from the start she's the Groom Killer, and now she's gone and murdered someone else. When are you people going to do your jobs?"

Brayden sucked in a breath, and Micah glanced over to see that his friend was on the verge of an explosion. Brayden's face had turned dark red, and his body was tense with anger. Micah put a restraining hand on Brayden's forearm, hoping he wouldn't lose his temper. If he lashed out at his uncle, Fenwick was just spiteful enough to take the matter up the chain of command and Brayden could very well lose his job.

Finn appeared to recognize the gravity of the situation as well, and he moved forward, forcing Fenwick back a step and blocking Brayden's view of their uncle. "Mister Colton," he said sharply. "You are interfering in official police business. Unless you want to be brought up on charges, I suggest you walk away and keep your opinions on this matter to yourself."

Fenwick blinked at his nephew's tone. "You wouldn't dare," he said. But there was a flicker of fear in his eyes that belied his apparent confidence.

Finn leaned in close. "Try me," he said softly.

Micah bit back a grin as Fenwick paled. He shot a hateful glare at Micah before retreating a few steps, turning his focus to the TV mounted in the far corner of the waiting room.

The elevator at the end of the hall dinged again, and Bea's sisters Layla, Gemma and Patience walked out. Patience, the veterinarian at the K-9 training center, gave him a nod as the group walked over to their father, and Micah relaxed a bit. Bea's siblings should be able to handle Fenwick, at least for the time being.

"Nice job, chief," Micah muttered.

Finn sighed. "I'm sure I'll pay for that later."

Micah noticed a doctor enter Bea's room and wondered if everything was okay. Had her injuries been more severe than they appeared? The gash on her forehead was deep and jagged, but Micah was more worried about a concussion or brain injury. She'd seemed to have no trouble speaking to him earlier, but he knew her head had been hurting. Hopefully that wasn't a sign of more serious damage.

He was so distracted he didn't realize Finn was

speaking to him until the man touched his shoulder. "Still with us?"

Micah shook his head. "Yes. Sorry. Uh, what were you saying?"

Finn lifted one eyebrow but didn't otherwise comment. "Ballistics probably won't be back until tomorrow afternoon. In the meantime, I want you to assume these two bodies are linked. I want you and Carson and Shane to coordinate your investigations until we know more."

"Yes, sir." Micah nodded. The door to Bea's room opened, and the doctor walked out. "I'll take care of it," he said, already walking toward the man in the white coat.

"Doctor?" The man turned. Micah showed him his badge. "I'm the officer who came in with Beatrix Colton. How is she?"

"She's got a mild concussion, but she should make a full recovery. I'm going to write up her discharge paperwork."

"Can I question her now?"

"I see no reason why not. But she might not be in the mood to talk. She's got a pretty severe headache."

Micah frowned, unhappy at the idea of Bea in pain. "Can you give her something for it?"

The doctor nodded. "Already ordered. It won't affect her cognitive abilities, so she should be able to answer questions if it's necessary."

"It is," Micah replied. The sooner he discovered what Bea had seen, the better his chances of catching whoever had attacked her. They'd been looking for a break in the Groom Killer investigation, and Bea might have just the information they needed to crack the case wide open.

Micah thanked the doctor and took a deep breath. He felt a fluttering sensation in his stomach, and he realized with a small shock that he was nervous. *Stop being ridiculous*, he told himself. He'd done well over a hundred interviews with witness and suspects alike since joining the Red Ridge police department. In all that time, he'd never once felt uncertain or worried before starting the process. Why was he acting like a rookie on his first day now?

Because it's Bea. The answer came immediately to his mind, and much as he wanted to deny it, he knew it was the truth. Bea Colton had always been his weakness, and even though years had passed since he'd seen her, his body still reacted the same way it always had to her presence.

Her father's words echoed in his mind. *Didn't you figure out she doesn't want you?*

"Oh, yes," he muttered. "She made that very clear."

Even now, the memory of her letter was enough to make his heart ache and his eyes sting. He'd looked for her letters at every mail call, but she'd never written. He'd told himself she was busy making their wedding plans and packing her things to join him after he returned. There was a lot to arrange while he was gone, and he felt guilty leaving her to do the lion's share of the work. But she had probably employed her grandmother's help, drawing on the older woman's expertise to plan a sweet, simple ceremony.

He'd been allowed one phone call after arriving at boot camp, but Bea hadn't been home. Normally, the lack of contact with her would have driven him crazy, but they kept him so busy he fell exhausted into his bed every night, too tired to do more than imagine her face before he drifted off to sleep.

Today was different though. There had been a letter for him at mail call, and once he saw the writing on the envelope, he knew it was from Bea. He'd have recognized her handwriting anywhere. Unable to wait for a little privacy, Micah had ripped open the letter then and there, only to crumple it in his hands a few seconds later.

Dear Micah,

I'm sorry to do this, but I've done a lot of thinking since you've been gone. I've decided that I'm not willing to be a soldier's wife. I want a husband who will be home every night, not someone who will be gone for months at a time. I know this probably comes as a shock, but being away from you has given me the time and space I needed to think. I rushed into our engagement, and now I realize it was a mistake.

Please don't try to contact me. I'm not going to change my mind.

Bea

Micah rubbed his chest to soothe the familiar ache. The pang of sadness had grown duller over the years, but any time he thought of Bea and the way she'd rejected him, his heart throbbed like a fresh bruise.

Part of him wondered if Fenwick was right. Perhaps he should recuse himself from the investigation and let someone else interview Bea. It would be easier than subjecting himself to the torture of being around her again, of hearing her voice and smelling her scent. He'd spent countless nights in the desert, dreaming of her and wishing he was holding her in his arms instead of snuggling with his service dog. Duke had been an exceptional military working dog, but he was a poor substitute for the woman Micah loved.

Because even though she'd broken his heart, Micah hadn't stopped loving Bea. And now that he'd seen her again, he realized he probably never would.

"A mild concussion," Bea said softly. She reached up to gently probe the gauze covering the gash on her forehead and exhaled heavily. "Could have been much worse, I guess."

Maybe she should close the shop for the next few days. After all, it wasn't like she had an army of brides beating down her door to buy wedding dresses. A little break might do her some good and give her the time and space to come up with a strategy for saving the shop.

A soft knock on the door interrupted her thoughts. "Come in," she called. Hopefully it was a nurse bringing the medication for her headache. Dimming the lights had helped dull the pain somewhat, but Bea wasn't going to turn down a little pharmaceutical assistance.

Micah poked his head around the door, and her heart did a little flip at the sight of him. "Mind if I come in?"

He looked shy and a little uncertain, and she felt a pang of worry. Had something happened between Micah and her father? She hadn't heard a loud commotion, but that didn't necessarily mean anything.

Micah entered the room and closed the door softly behind him. "The doctor said you'll be released soon."

"I hope so." Right now, she wanted nothing more than to go home and lie down in her own bed. Hopefully she'd feel better after a good night's sleep.

"Do you feel up to talking while we wait for your discharge orders to go through?"

Now it was her turn to feel hesitant. "Okay," she said. Did he really want to discuss their past right now? She didn't think it was the best time, but perhaps he had something to say after all these years...

"I need you to walk me through what happened at the boutique tonight. Do you remember seeing or hearing anything unusual before you were attacked?"

Of course, she thought, feeling ridiculous. Micah wasn't here to talk about their past. He wanted to know about the events that had landed her in the hospital. He was a police officer, after all, and was only talking to her as part of his duties. Seeing her again had probably not affected him the same way it had her.

And why would it? He'd been the one to break up

with her. It only made sense that he'd moved on with his life in the years since she'd received his letter. The thought of Micah with another woman left her feeling mildly nauseous and she swallowed hard. *It doesn't matter,* she told herself. *It's none of my business.*

It was the truth, but a pang of jealousy speared her heart as the image of him holding another woman flashed through her mind. Micah's actions had hurt her badly, and yet she couldn't deny she still felt drawn to him.

"Bea?" The sound of her name drew her out of her thoughts, and she focused on Micah to find he was watching her with a concerned expression. "If you're not feeling up to it, I can talk to you later."

"No, now is fine." Better to get this over with so she could simply go home. "I was closing up the store when I heard a strange thump in the storage room." She told him about how the lights had gone out as she'd headed to the back of the store and the strange smell in the air. "I heard the sound of movement, and the next thing I remember is you leaning over me, telling me to wake up."

Micah frowned. "Can you describe the scent?"

"It was definitely perfume," Bea responded. "Something floral, but with a sharp note to it that burned my nose."

"Did you recognize it?"

Bea tilted her head to the side. "It seemed familiar, but I don't remember where I've encountered it before." She searched her memory, but it was no use.

Finally, she shrugged. "Maybe I smelled it as I walked by the perfume counter at the mall?"

"It's possible," Micah said. "When you're feeling up to it, we'll go there and see if you can identify it for me."

Before she could reply, Micah asked another question. "Did you see anything in the darkness?"

Bea closed her eyes, thinking back to that moment. "Just a shadowy form. I couldn't make out any real details."

"Was it bigger or smaller than you?" Micah probed.

"About my height," she said. "Maybe a little shorter?"

He nodded, as if she'd just confirmed something for him. "Did they say anything or make any kind of sound before hitting you?"

"No." She saw his mouth tighten, and realized she wasn't being very helpful. "I'm sorry," she said. "It all happened so fast, and I really couldn't see much of anything with the lights out."

"This is fine," he said, flashing a quick smile. "Are you absolutely certain the store was empty when you heard the sound in the back room?"

"Well, I *thought* I was alone," Bea said, frowning. "But that clearly wasn't the case."

Micah made a thoughtful sound low in his throat. "Do you think a customer snuck into the back room while you weren't looking?"

"No. I only had three customers yesterday, and I watched them all leave." *Former customers*, she amended silently, as all three women had come to either cancel their dress orders or return a dress they'd previously purchased.

"All right." He ran a hand through his hair, mussing the auburn strands. "We'll need to keep your store closed tomorrow so the evidence techs can finish processing the scene—"

"Wait...what?" That seemed like a lot of trouble for what amounted to a hit-and-run attack.

Micah frowned, as if confused by her reaction. Then realization dawned in his eyes and his expression cleared. "You don't know," he said softly. "How could you?"

"Know what?" Bea asked. Her stomach churned uneasily at this sudden turn in the conversation. Something else had happened in the store, and given Micah's reaction, it wasn't good.

He took her hand, and she felt the calluses on his palm. "We found another Groom Killer victim in one of the dressing rooms." His voice was soft, belying the horror of his words.

Bea felt the blood drain from her head. "What?" she whispered. Surely there had been some mistake. If word got out that the Groom Killer had struck again, and in her own bridal boutique, no less, her business would never recover.

Guilt flashed through her at the selfish thought and she shook her head. "Who?"

Micah didn't need her to elaborate. "We think it's Joey McBurn."

Bea closed her eyes, picturing Joey's fiancée. Angelina Cooper had come into the shop a few months ago, bubbling with excitement. Joey had just proposed, and Angelina was wasting no time planning their wedding. She'd tried on several dresses, but unfortunately, her tastes ran to the expensive and she hadn't been able to afford her dream dress. Bea had tried to steer her to a similar, less pricey style, but Angelina hadn't budged. She'd left the store, swearing she'd be back once she'd saved up enough money. She must have found something at the department store in town, because the wedding was tomorrow.

Or at least, it should have been.

Bea's heart went out to the other woman. Did she even know Joey was dead? Or was she waiting at home, expecting him to walk through the door at any moment?

Micah leaned forward, his hand tightening on hers. "You're the first person to encounter the Groom Killer and live to talk about it," he said quietly. "I want to put you in protective custody, to make sure you're safe in case the killer targets you again."

Bea's heart began to pound. "Do you really think that's a possibility?" The Groom Killer went after men, not women. And she hadn't seen anything in the dark—surely the killer would know Bea couldn't identify them.

"I think it's a risk we can't afford to take." He gave her hand a final squeeze and released it, and Bea immediately missed the warmth of his touch. "I can start the paperwork—"

"That won't be necessary."

Disappointment flashed across Micah's face. "Bea, please," he began, but she lifted her hand to cut him off.

"I'll agree to a bodyguard, but only under one condition."

"What's that?" There was a note of wariness in his voice, as if he was worried about what she was going to say.

"It's got to be you," Bea said firmly. "No one else."

"Me?" Micah made a strangled sound, and Bea fought the urge to laugh. She knew how ridiculous her request must seem to him. They hadn't seen each other in years, and after the way he'd ended things between them, he probably figured she wanted nothing more to do with him.

Truth be told, Bea herself was surprised by the intensity of her determination. But she felt safe with Micah, and she knew he would protect her if the Groom Killer did come back around. Besides, maybe if they spent more time together she could finally get him out of her system and truly move on. The man had flaws—he was only human, after all. Hopefully seeing them up close again would be enough to take the shine off of her memories of their time together.

It was a long shot, but she was just desperate enough to take it.

Chapter 4

Micah stood frozen in place, too stunned to do much more than blink at Bea as he processed her words.

"You want me to…guard you?" He spoke slowly, hoping that Bea would really listen to his words and see her request for what it was.

A mistake.

She nodded, her expression determined. "That's right."

It was the concussion talking—that had to be it. Why else would she want him to protect her? Her letter had made it very clear she was finished with him, so why would she suddenly change her mind?

Micah shook his head. He could worry about her motivations later. Right now, he had to make her see reason.

"I don't think that's such a good idea," he began. "We have officers who are more experienced in protection work, including several women. It would be better if you agreed to let one of them guard you. Much easier for everyone involved."

Bea met his gaze, her hazel eyes clear. "I trust you," she said simply. "You're the only one I feel safe with."

Maybe you shouldn't, he thought darkly. People had trusted him before, and it had ended badly.

Micah closed his eyes, bracing himself against the onslaught of memories washing over him.

Afghanistan. Helmand Province. Micah and Duke had been deployed with a squad of marines and Afghan army troops to comb through the rubble of a drone attack in search of the bodies of a local Taliban warlord and his cronies. It was supposed to be a training exercise, of sorts, with the Afghan army troops taking the lead in the search while Micah and the marines provided guidance and cover.

Things had started out well enough. Micah and the marines had established a perimeter around the site so the Afghan troops could work in relative safety. It had been shaping up to be just another search, until one of the troops asked Micah for assistance. He and Duke had left their position, and that's when the ambush had started.

A hail of bullets had erupted with no warning, cutting down several Afghan troops and pinning the marines and Micah in place. The fighting had been brutal and fierce, and several marines had been injured.

Including Duke.

Micah could still hear the dog's pained yelp and the sounds of his whimpering as he'd lain in the dirt at Micah's feet.

Unable to bear the dog's suffering, Micah had slowed his return fire so he could attend to Duke's injuries. And that's when the man next to him had been hit.

After an eternity of fighting, reinforcements had arrived and the insurgents had been beaten back or killed. Medics had poured in, attending to the wounded. Duke had been placed on a stretcher and airlifted along with the rest of the injured, Micah by his side the whole way.

In the end, Duke had survived his wound and retired a hero. One of the veterinary nurses who cared for him fell in love with him, and Duke now lived a life of ease with the woman and her family. It was the best possible outcome for the dog, but Micah still couldn't shake the guilt that plagued him whenever he thought of that day.

If I hadn't left my position...if I hadn't stopped to tend to Duke... How many people would still be alive if Micah had made different decisions? How many bodies would have remained whole and unbroken if Micah hadn't left a gap in the coverage, not once, but twice?

The after-action review had found no fault, but

deep in his gut Micah knew things would have turned out differently if he'd made other choices.

With his partner in the hospital, Micah had felt like an amputee. The military had offered to pair him with another dog, but Micah had refused. It took months of intense training to bond with a dog, and Micah didn't have it in him to go through the experience again. He'd known that if he lost another animal, it would break him.

It turned out that fate had other plans. When he'd taken the job in Red Ridge, the thought of pairing with another dog had worried him. But as soon as he'd met Chunk, his heart had embraced the animal without reservation.

"Micah?" Bea's voice cut through his thoughts, drawing him back to the present. "Are you okay? You look like you're going to be sick."

He nodded, shaking off the sadness and despair of his memories. "I'm fine," he replied. "Just thinking."

Bea was quiet a moment. "I'm not trying to be difficult," she said. "And I know this is awkward. But you're the only one I trust. Will you please work with me?"

Micah let out a heavy sigh. "All right," he said. "I'll do it." He'd probably come to regret his decision, but Micah knew Bea was a stubborn woman. If she said she wouldn't allow anyone else to guard her, she meant it. And since Micah couldn't leave her unprotected, he didn't have many other options.

A sharp knock sounded in the room, and the door

swung open. "You've been in here long enough," Fenwick snapped. "I need to see my daughter."

Micah bit his tongue to keep from responding as Bea's siblings filed in behind their father. Patience offered him an apologetic glance and reached out to touch Fenwick's arm.

"Dad," she said. "We can't interrupt Micah's interview. It's inappropriate."

"It's fine," Fenwick said. "Anything Bea has to say, she can say in front of us."

"I'm done for now," Micah said. He turned to Bea. "I'll start making the necessary arrangements."

She nodded. "Thank you."

"Arrangements for what?" Fenwick sounded irate. "I can take care of anything you need. There's no reason he should be involved."

Bea glanced at her father, and Micah recognized the glint of steel in her eyes. *Oh, boy*, he thought. *Things are about to get interesting.*

"Micah is going to act as my protection until this case is closed," she said calmly. "We agreed it was the best course of action, given the circumstances."

"What?" Fenwick's face turned an unhealthy-looking shade of purple, and Micah eyed the emergency call button on the wall. It wouldn't surprise him if the older man had a rage stroke on the spot.

"You heard me," Bea said calmly. If she was upset by her father's reaction, she didn't show it. Then again, she'd been dealing with the man her entire life. She'd probably learned a few tricks for handling him in that time.

Apparently, her siblings had, as well. They moved forward as a group, each one speaking in low, soothing tones as they circled their father.

Fenwick ignored them, his gaze locked on Bea. "Absolutely not," he said in a low voice. "I forbid it."

Bea arched one eyebrow. "I wasn't asking for your permission."

"You don't know what you're saying." Fenwick's voice softened, as if he were speaking to a child. "You've had a bad scare and a nasty bump on the head. You're not thinking rationally."

"I know what I'm doing," Bea replied.

Her father tried another tack. "I can arrange for you to have a bodyguard, if that will make you feel better. I'll even get you set up in a temporary apartment. Let's just talk this over like two adults, and I'm sure we can figure out a way to keep you safe without making any…rash decisions."

"Dad—" Patience tried to interject, but Fenwick waved his daughter away.

"This is between me and your sister," he said firmly.

Bea sighed heavily. "No, it isn't. There's nothing for us to discuss. I can see you're upset, but I've made up my mind and I'm not going to change it. Accept it or don't—I really don't care either way."

Admiration swelled in Micah's chest, and for a moment, he was proud of Bea for standing up to her father. She'd always had an independent streak, but back when they were dating, she'd sometimes had trouble going against her father's wishes. That didn't seem to be the case anymore, and Micah was happy to see Bea wasn't living under Fenwick's thumb.

Fenwick straightened his shoulders. "I'm going to pretend your insolence is due to your injuries," he said stiffly.

Bea shrugged. "Okay."

Patience placed her hand on her father's arm, and one of her sisters did the same on Fenwick's other side. "Let's go," Patience said softly. "Bea needs her rest."

Fenwick shook off the touch of his children and straightened his tie. "Yes, I'm sure she does." He smoothed a hand over his suit jacket, then leaned forward and pressed a kiss to Bea's forehead. "I'll check on you later. I expect you'll be back to yourself by then."

Without another word, Fenwick turned on his heel and stalked out the door. The room seemed to deflate after he left, the tension dropping dramatically in the wake of his exit. As if responding to some invisible signal, Bea's siblings moved as a group to surround her bed. They began talking to her in low, soothing tones, and Micah could tell by the way Bea's features relaxed that she was happy to see her sisters.

He moved quietly toward the door, wanting to give the family some privacy. The thought that Fenwick might be lurking in the hallway gave him pause, but he cast off the concern and left the room. He'd actually rather face the mayor than infringe on Bea's time with her siblings.

Fortunately, the older man was nowhere to be found, so Micah finally had a moment's peace to think.

He walked over to the small waiting area just down the hall from Bea's room and sat, his mind racing. How in the world was he going to protect Bea when there was so much left unsaid between them? He knew from experience how dangerous it was to be distracted on a mission, and he wasn't sure he could simply set aside his emotions where Bea was concerned. Could he stand to be around her, knowing his heart had never really moved on?

But could he risk saying no? Bea had made it very clear she'd only cooperate if he acted as her protection. If he didn't at least try to push his emotions aside, Bea wouldn't have anyone looking out for her.

The thought of Bea in the crosshairs of the Groom Killer was enough to strengthen Micah's resolve. Right now, she was the best lead they had in this case, and he owed it to the people of Red Ridge to do whatever he could to bring the Groom Killer to justice. If that meant spending time with Bea, then that's what he would do.

Hopefully his heart would understand.

Maybe this isn't such a good idea, after all…

An orderly had helped Bea into a wheelchair and had taken her as far as the hospital entrance. Micah had taken it from there, pushing her through the dark parking lot and over to his car.

"Almost there," he said quietly.

The evening air was cool, and she could feel his

body heat at her back, enveloping her like a comforting blanket. The hospital had planted rose bushes around the building, and their perfume filled the air. But Bea could still smell Micah's scent—warm, male skin, some kind of woodsy soap and the barest hint of laundry detergent. It filled her head and made her feel soft inside.

Am I really going to be able to handle being around him 24/7?

It was something she should have thought about before she'd made her knee-jerk decision. But when Micah had told her she was a possible target of the Groom Killer, she'd acted out of fear. Micah had always made her feel safe, and that hadn't changed in the years since they'd been apart. Her insistence on his being the one to guard her was an instinctive reaction, and she hadn't stopped to consider the consequences for her heart.

It's just a job to him, she reminded herself. Micah had only agreed to protect her because he was working on the Groom Killer case. As long as Bea remembered that, she might be able to get through this with her dignity intact.

"Here we are." Micah stopped next to a dark SUV, and Bea noticed the windows were down. "Let me get you settled in the front, and then I'll take care of Chunk."

"Chunk?" Bea echoed. But as soon as Micah opened the passenger door, she understood.

A basset hound was curled up on the backseat, looking quite at home in a nest of blankets. "Oh, hello," she said, a little surprised at the unexpected sight.

The dog lifted his head and regarded her curiously. He sniffed at the air and, apparently finding her harmless, laid his head back down on his paws.

Micah helped Bea to stand. "That's my partner," he explained as he guided her into the passenger seat.

Bea was so distracted by the dog she was surprised by the feel of Micah's hands on her skin. Even though there was nothing personal about his touch, her body still responded, sending sparks down her limbs.

"I didn't know you worked with a dog."

"Yep." Micah pulled the seatbelt out for her, and she buckled herself in. "I'm with the K-9 Unit. Chunk's a cadaver dog, trained to find bodies. He's actually the one who found you."

Bea frowned. "But I'm not dead."

A shadow crossed Micah's face, barely visible in the glow of the streetlight. "No, thankfully you're not." He shook his head, as if to cast off a bad mood. "Chunk is actually trained to detect blood, so sometimes he'll find a victim who is still alive. Like you." He offered her a tight smile before shutting the door.

Bea twisted around to regard the dog as Micah opened the back door. "Then I guess you're the one I really need to thank," she said.

Chunk lifted his head again, his dark brown eyes gentle. He turned to nose Micah, who was busy dumping a bowl of kibble into a storage bin. "Has he been here all evening?"

"Yeah," Micah responded, turning to dump out a

bowl of water. "He's used to hanging out in the SUV if I go somewhere that isn't too dog friendly."

"Aren't you worried about him getting too hot?"

"Not in this weather," Micah said. "It's still cool enough that when I park in the shade with the windows down he does okay. I don't leave him alone if it's warm outside. It's not worth the risk." He stretched his arm out, handing her something small. "Here. He's usually pretty friendly, but if you give him this he'll be your best friend forever."

Bea glanced at the object to find Micah had passed her a dog treat. She laughed softly. "Fair enough." She reached into the backseat, extending the gift. Chunk took one sniff and leaned forward, retrieving the biscuit from her hand in one surprisingly delicate bite. His breath was humid on her hand, and he gave her a quick swipe with his tongue as if to say thanks.

Micah climbed behind the steering wheel and started the engine. "Ready?"

Bea wasn't sure if he was talking to her or the dog, so she answered for the both of them. "Yes."

He put the truck in gear, then stopped and turned to her with a worried look. "Uh, you're not allergic to dogs, are you?"

"No," she replied.

Relief flashed across his face and he returned his attention to driving. "That's good," he said. "I hadn't thought to ask you about it before."

"I take it Chunk is your roommate?"

"Something like that," Micah said, turning on to the main street in front of the hospital. "Mostly, though, I'm more like his servant." He didn't sound like he was bothered by this arrangement, and Bea smiled.

"Sounds like a good deal for Chunk." She glanced back at the dog, who was stretched out on the seat again. He was longer than she'd expected, but then again, Bea had never been around a basset hound before.

"Trust me, he's got nothing to complain about."

"Except for maybe his name," Bea remarked. "Chunk isn't a very dignified name."

The dog in question snorted, as if agreeing with her.

"Well, that's more of a nickname," Micah said. "His given name is Chase, but no one ever calls him that."

"Too bad," Bea said. "It's a nice name."

"It is," Micah agreed. "But you have to admit, he is a little…stout."

"That's hardly his fault," she protested.

Micah laughed softly. "You don't have to defend him to me," he said. "I love the guy. And if I thought his nickname actually hurt his feelings, I wouldn't use it. But believe it or not, he won't answer to Chase. He only responds to Chunk."

The dog snorted again, confirming his master's words.

"How long have you two worked together?" She was genuinely curious, and Micah's relationship with Chunk seemed like a fairly safe topic of conversation.

"Almost two years. I was partnered with him right after I joined the force."

"Did you always know you wanted to have a dog as a partner?" It wasn't the usual career path for a police officer, but then again, Red Ridge was known for its K-9 police unit and dog training center, courtesy of her father's money. It was one of the more unselfish things Fenwick had done, and if it hadn't been for her mother's insistence, he probably wouldn't have even considered it.

Micah was quiet, and for a moment Bea wondered if he was going to answer the question. She didn't think it was too personal, but perhaps he didn't want to talk about his motivations for joining the K-9 squad. "I actually worked with a dog while I was in the Army Rangers. His name was Duke, and he was a German shepherd."

"Was?" She picked up on the past tense of the word, and her stomach tightened. Had something happened to the dog? No wonder Micah didn't want to discuss it…

"Duke was shot during an ambush. Fortunately, he survived, and one of the veterinary nurses who took care of him adopted him."

Bea breathed a sigh of relief at hearing the dog was okay. "That must have been really difficult, seeing him injured like that."

"Yeah." Micah swallowed hard. "It was one of the lowest moments of my life."

Silence fell over them, and Bea could have kicked

herself for pressing for more information. So much for keeping the conversation light and easy.

Bea searched for something to say but came up empty. She wished they could go back to the easy back-and-forth of a moment ago, but she couldn't think of another topic of conversation to try. So she remained quiet, figuring it was better to say nothing at all than to blurt out something she'd come to regret.

Micah seemed comfortable with the silence, and she had to wonder if maybe he preferred it to talking to her. After all, he'd left her once before. He probably would have been happy to carry on without her in his life, but she'd forced her way back in, if only for a little while.

The thought had her second-guessing her decision once more, and she shifted in the seat. "How long do you think this will last?"

Micah lifted one shoulder in a shrug as he considered her question. "I'm not sure. Maybe a few days. Possibly longer than that."

Bea frowned, turning to look out the window so he wouldn't catch her expression. While a part of her was uncomfortable with the idea of spending so much time with Micah, a larger part insisted she stay with him. It didn't make sense, but with the rest of her world in such chaos, she wanted—no, *needed*— the comfort of the familiar. And even though she and Micah had spent a lot of time apart, she still felt like she knew him. He was a safe port in this storm, and she wasn't strong enough to pretend otherwise.

"I'm going to keep you safe," he said quietly. "I

know things are…different…between us, but I won't let you get hurt again."

"I know," she said, turning back to offer him a small smile. "I trust you, Micah. That's why I was so insistent in the hospital."

He opened his mouth to respond, but apparently thought better of it. He cleared his throat, instead, leaving her wondering what he'd left unsaid.

"Micah?"

"We're almost home," he said, dodging her implicit question.

Bea leaned back against the headrest, knowing better than to pry. It was only natural he was quiet around her. They were still getting used to seeing each other again.

He turned onto a graveled drive, and she glanced out the window at the trees that dotted the landscape. It wasn't until they were halfway down the drive that she realized she knew where they were headed because she'd been there before.

"This might be my concussion talking, but are we going to your aunt's house?"

Micah gave her a fleeting smile. "Yeah. At least, it was her house. She left it to me after she died."

Bea vaguely remembered reading the woman's obituary in the local paper several years ago. Micah had still been deployed, and she'd meant to go to the funeral to pay her respects. But something had come up, and she hadn't made it to the service.

"I was sorry to hear of her passing."

"Thank you." He was quiet a moment as they

crunched along the drive. "It was rough on me, losing her. We were close, and I hated not being able to come home to see her before she died."

Bea hadn't known the woman had been sick until the announcement of her death. Micah's Aunt Wanda had been a friendly yet private woman, and like many other people her age, she had had her pride. It would never have occurred to her to ask for help, and Bea felt a little stab of guilt for not checking on her while Micah was away.

"I'm sure she understood," Bea said. "I know she was very proud of you." Bea wasn't just trying to make Micah feel better. She'd spent some time with Aunt Wanda when she and Micah had dated, and the woman's love for her nephew had been obvious enough for a blind man to see. Micah's aunt hadn't been able to have children of her own, so she was practically a second mother to Micah, especially after his own had died when he was only twelve.

Bea reached out in the darkness of the truck and laid her hand on his forearm. He jumped, clearly startled by her touch. But a second later his hand slid over hers, large and warm and a little rough against her skin.

For a moment, Bea allowed herself to pretend they were still a couple, headed home after a nice evening out in Red Ridge. She pictured a gold band on her hand, his matching ring glinting in the moonlight shining through the driver's side window. Their kids would be tucked into bed by now, the sitter watching something on TV with the volume down low. They'd walk into the house and Chunk would rise from his bed in the kitchen to greet them and beg for a treat. They'd pay the babysitter and check on the kids, one boy and one girl, then head to their bedroom and make love before falling asleep in each other's arms.

It was an image that made her heart ache. How different her life would have been, if only Micah hadn't changed his mind. It was on the tip of her tongue to ask him why, but the idea of having that conversation was overwhelming, especially with her current headache.

A moment later, Micah pulled into the paved driveway and parked the truck under a large carport. He killed the engine, then turned to Bea. "Wait here," he said softly. "I'll come around to help you out."

Bea nodded, grateful for his offer. She was still a little unsteady on her feet, and it bothered her to feel so weak. Her doctor had assured her it was normal, and told her the sensation would soon pass. Bea hoped he was right—she couldn't very well spend the next few days literally leaning on Micah whenever she needed to walk somewhere.

Micah hopped out of the truck and opened the back door. Bea heard a scraping sound and looked back to see he'd dragged a small ramp across the concrete, fitting it against the seat. Chunk waited until his master pointed to the ramp and then scampered down with slightly more grace than Bea had expected. Once his paws hit the ground, Micah pulled the ramp away from the truck and shut the door.

Man and dog rounded the hood together and came

to stand by the passenger door. Bea felt a little self-conscious being the focus of so much attention, but as soon as Micah touched her hand the sensation fled. He helped her slide out of the truck and tucked her hand into the crook of his arm as they started down the short walk to the front door. Chunk fell into step on Bea's other side so she was flanked by the two males. Even though Chunk's head only came up to her knee, Bea knew he would do everything in his power to help keep her steady, and she felt a surge of affection for the dog. She'd never really considered herself an animal person before, but she might have to make an exception for Chunk.

The house was orderly, but a thin veneer of dust on some of the tables was a testament to Micah's workload. He led her down the main hallway to a bedroom in the back of the house and indicated a chair in the corner of the room. Bea sat, Chunk at her feet, while Micah quickly stripped the bed and put on fresh linens.

Bea glanced around, trying to determine if this was Micah's room or simply a guest room. She wasn't about to displace him from his own bed.

She didn't see any personal effects in the room, but Micah had always been tidy, and his time in the army had probably reinforced the habit. A few pictures hung on the walls, framed shots of sunrises and sunsets in a desert, the sky a kaleidoscope of oranges and pinks and reds that looked too intense to be real. "These photos are gorgeous," she said.

Micah glanced up and smiled. "Thanks. I took

them while I was on deployment. Photography was kind of a hobby for me then."

"What about now?" Bea was no art critic, but based on those shots it seemed like Micah had real talent. It would be a shame for him to let it lie dormant.

He shrugged as he folded an extra blanket and placed it at the foot of the bed. "I don't get out with my camera as much as I used to. There just hasn't been time."

"That's too bad," she remarked. "Hopefully after you close the Groom Killer case your schedule will go back to normal."

"That would be nice," Micah said. "You're all set in here. Let me show you the bathroom, and I'll grab a spare T-shirt and some flannel pants for you to sleep in tonight."

For the first time, Bea realized she didn't have any of her clothes or toiletries. "Do you think we can stop by my place tomorrow so I can pack a bag?" she asked as she followed him down the hallway again.

"No problem." Micah showed her the bathroom and placed some clean towels and a few sample containers of soap, shampoo and toothpaste on the counter, along with a travel-size toothbrush that was still in its original wrapper.

"Thank you," she said, touched by his willingness to welcome her into his home. Would she have been so gracious if the shoe had been on the other foot? "I'm not staying in your bedroom, am I? I don't want you to give up your bed for me."

Micah shook his head. "You're in the guest room.

I'm just down the hall, across from you." He studied her face. "You look tired." It wasn't a compliment, but his voice was kind. "Are you hungry? I can fix a sandwich or heat a can of soup if you'd like something to eat."

Bea hadn't eaten since lunch, but the thought of food made her stomach roll. "No, thanks. I think I'd rather just wash up and go to bed, if that's okay with you."

The corner of Micah's mouth curved up. "You don't have to keep me entertained," he said. "We'll leave you to it, then. Holler at me if you need anything." He and Chunk backed out of the room and into the hall.

"Thank you," Bea called out. He acknowledged her words with a wave of his hand as he and the dog walked toward the kitchen. Bea closed the door and turned to the sink, wincing as she caught sight of her reflection in the mirror.

A large bandage dominated her forehead, a few spots of red bright on the white gauze. She poked gingerly at the area, but it was still numb from the injections the doctor had administered before he'd stitched her up.

"That's going to hurt in the morning," she muttered. And it wasn't going to be pretty, either. But she'd take a gash on the head over being dead any day.

It didn't take long to carefully splash water on her face and brush her teeth. A few minutes later, Bea stepped out into the hall and made her way back to the guest bedroom.

A folded shirt and pair of pants had been set on the bed, and for a moment, Bea could only stare at them. She had no doubt they'd fit her—actually, given Micah's size, his clothes would be quite large on her. But the idea of wearing his shirt gave her pause. It was such an intimate act—the kind of thing lovers did without a second thought. Once upon a time, she would have slipped on his shirt without hesitation. Now she wasn't so sure…

She didn't have many other options, though. She couldn't sleep in her clothes; she had to wear them again tomorrow and didn't want to wrinkle them too badly. And sleeping nude was out of the question. With her luck, the smoke alarm would go off in the middle of the night and she'd spring from bed, forgetting her lack of clothes.

There was no help for it. She was going to have to wear Micah's shirt.

Bea undressed and draped her clothes across the back of the chair. Then she tugged the gray shirt over her head.

As she'd thought, it was large on her, the hem falling midway to her knees and the sleeves ending past her elbows. It was also incredibly soft and smelled strongly of Micah's detergent. She took a deep breath before she could stop herself, savoring the scent she'd always associated with him.

The sheets were cool as she slid into bed, and for the first time since her attack, Bea's body relaxed completely, sinking into the embrace of the soft mattress. Bea normally had trouble falling asleep in a new place, but that wasn't going to be a problem tonight. She turned onto her side and wrapped her arms around herself, breathing in the comforting scent of the man she loved as exhaustion claimed her.

Chapter 5

Micah woke to the feel of a cold, wet nose in his ear. He turned on his side to find Chunk regarding him solemnly, his front paws braced on the mattress.

"That time already?"

Chunk nosed him again, and swiped his tongue across Micah's chin. "Okay, okay, I'm awake."

Micah rubbed the grit from his eyes and forced himself to sit up, knowing that if he continued to lay there he'd fall asleep again. He wasn't usually a morning person, and his time in the army hadn't changed that. But it was tougher than usual to get up today. He hadn't slept well the night before. His body had been very aware of Bea's presence on the other side of the hall, and he'd been unable to fully relax. He'd finally given in to fatigue around four in the morning, which made Chunk's regular 7:00 a.m. wake-up call especially painful.

He pulled on a pair of pajama pants and made a quick stop in the attached bathroom before opening his bedroom door. The smell hit him as soon as he stepped into the hallway. Coffee. Fresh and hot.

Micah's stomach roared to life, and he glanced at the door to the guest bedroom. It was still closed, but Bea had to be awake. She was probably starving, since she'd turned down his offer of a quick meal the night before. He hurried down the hall, hoping she'd been able to find something to eat.

He stepped into the kitchen and drew up short at the sight that greeted him. Bea was in front of the stove, scrambling eggs from the smell of things. Her hair was pulled back in a messy ponytail, and she looked adorably sexy in his T-shirt and pajama pants. They hung off her slender frame, obscuring her curves, but he still found the image appealing. His throat tightened as he realized this would have been his life if she hadn't chosen another path. It was a welcome sight to wake up to, but he forced himself to look away. Not a day went by that Micah didn't wish things had turned out differently, but he couldn't torture himself by dwelling on things that would never come to pass.

Chunk nudged his knee, and Micah realized he'd forgotten all about his partner. "Good morning," he called out, not wanting to sneak up on Bea.

She jumped and turned to face him, and he saw her toenails were painted a bright orange. It was such a departure from Bea's normally professional dress that it made him wonder what other frivolous things she might be hiding under those skirt suits she wore to work. Red lace bras? Black satin thongs? His mind quickly veered off into dangerous territory, and Micah swallowed hard as he tried to rein in his thoughts. The last thing he needed was to start fantasizing about Bea. Their relationship was always going to be impersonal, nothing more.

Too bad. Regret lanced through him and he pushed the feeling aside. He needed to focus on keeping Bea safe, and any extraneous emotions were only going to get in the way of his duty.

"Good morning," she said, offering him a smile. "I hope you don't mind, but I woke up early and decided to make breakfast."

Micah's usual fare was a cup of coffee and a bagel clenched between his teeth as he loaded Chunk into the truck. He told her as much and added, "I can already see you've far surpassed that."

"It's not that special," she replied, angling her body back to the stove so she could continue monitoring the eggs. "But I do like to cook."

"Seeing as how I like to eat, I think this will work out well."

Bea laughed softly, and Micah smiled, pleased she'd taken his comment in the spirit he'd intended it. "I need to let Chunk out. We'll be right back."

"This'll be ready in a few minutes. Take your time."

Micah opened the back door for his ever-patient

partner and stepped outside. The morning air was chilly, and the cold helped to clear his mind. He could already tell it was going to be difficult to walk the line between friendly and flirting when he spoke with Bea. The last time he'd seen her they'd been together, planning their future.

Despite the fact that she'd broken up with him, his body still retained the sense memory of their closeness, and he found himself slipping into old habits without realizing it. But they were two different people now, and even though being around her was like putting on an old pair of jeans, he had to remember they no longer had a relationship. He couldn't talk to her like an old friend, couldn't assume she would welcome that closeness and familiarity.

And, really, it was better for him to put up some barriers between them. His heart was already too involved—he could practically *feel* his interest in her blooming, like a new plant breaking free of its seed in search of the sun. He had to put the brakes on his emotions now, before he reached a point of no return.

Chunk trotted over, his business concluded. Micah grabbed the towel he kept on one of the porch chairs and wiped the dew off Chunk's coat. Being so low to the ground, the dog tended to get pretty wet during his morning tour of the yard, and Micah had learned it was easier to clean him off outside. Early on, he'd made the mistake of taking Chunk into the house in search of a towel, and his partner had wasted no time shaking the water droplets free, spraying the furniture and floor with moisture.

They stepped back into the warm house and headed for the kitchen. "Me, again," Micah said quietly as he walked to the pantry to retrieve the dog food.

"I heard you coming," Bea said. "But I do appreciate the heads-up."

He grabbed a bowl from the cupboard and began to pour the kibble. "I figured you might still be on edge from the attack last night. I don't want to scare you." He bent to put the bowl on the floor and straightened to find Bea watching him, a strange expression on her face. For a second, he thought he saw the glint of tears in her eyes, but then she blinked and the impression was gone.

"Thank you," she said softly. "That's very thoughtful of you."

Micah shrugged, her gratitude making him feel a little awkward. He didn't want her to think she needed to offer any kind of appreciation for his actions. If she started looking at him with stars in her eyes, it would be that much harder for him to keep his distance.

"Let me get the plates," he said, searching for a change of subject.

He set the table while Bea finished up at the stove. He poured them both a cup of coffee while Bea brought the pan of eggs and a plate of buttered toast to the table. "I didn't see any bacon," she said as she sat. "But I did add some cheese to the eggs."

"It looks amazing," Micah said. "I appreciate you going to all this trouble."

She waved away his comment. "Like I said, it's

nothing special. If you don't mind, I'll draw up a list for your next trip to the grocery store."

Visions of home-cooked meals danced in Micah's head, and he held back a groan. His dinners usually consisted of a frozen meal or a burger from the drive-through. It would be nice to have real food for a change.

But he couldn't get into the habit of letting Bea cook for him. She wasn't his wife or his girlfriend. She was his job.

"That won't be necessary," he said. Her face fell, and he realized his tone had been sharper than necessary. He took a sip of coffee and tried again. "I appreciate the offer, but you don't need to worry about cooking for me."

She opened her mouth to reply, but seemed to think better of it. They ate in silence for a few minutes, and Micah had to admit the eggs were wonderful.

"So, how does this work?" Bea asked. She forked the last bite of eggs into her mouth and looked at him expectantly.

"You mean your protection?"

She nodded, and he took a bite of eggs, thinking as he chewed.

"Well, it means I'm going to be your shadow for the foreseeable future. Wherever you go, I'll be there." He took a sip of coffee. "I don't have to follow you into the bathroom or anything, but I will be sticking close."

Bea frowned and wrapped her hands around her

mug. "But how will you get any work done if you're stuck babysitting me?"

He chuckled. "You are my work," he said simply.

Bea flushed, her cheeks turning pink as she digested his words. "Oh." She shifted in her chair. "I doubt you'll make much progress on the Groom Killer case if you're at the shop with me all day."

"It will make things a bit more difficult," he allowed. "But I can use my phone to stay in touch with the rest of the team."

Bea stood and began clearing the dishes. Micah pushed his chair back and headed for the sink. "You cooked, I'll clean."

She nodded and leaned against the counter, mug in hand. "Why don't we try this, instead? I'll work in the shop for a few hours in the mornings, and then we'll head to your office for the rest of the day."

Micah considered her suggestion as he scrubbed the pan. It would make his life easier if he could actually put some time in at the squad every day, but it couldn't be good for Bea's business if she cut hours.

"What about your shop?" he asked. "I'd hate for you to lose any customers because you changed your schedule."

"Don't worry about it," she replied. "Things have been really slow lately. The Groom Killer has everyone on edge, and lots of couples are canceling their weddings and returning their dresses. It might even turn out for the best," she said with a wry smile. "If the shop is closed most of the day, people can't ask for a refund."

Her tone was light, but Micah knew she was truly worried. All the more reason for him to accept her offer; the more time he spent working on the case, the faster he and the team would catch the Groom Killer and Bea's business would bounce back.

"Okay," he said, squeezing excess water from the sponge. "That sounds like a good plan."

Bea nodded and pushed off the counter. "Mind if I take the first shower? I'll be quick."

"No worries," Micah replied. "I sleep in the master suite, which has its own bathroom. You don't need to rush on my account."

"Good to know." Bea rinsed her cup and placed it in the dishwasher. "I'll see you in a bit, then." She set off down the hall, and Chunk trotted after her. The dog stopped in the doorway and glanced back at Micah, then turned to follow Bea.

"Traitor," Micah muttered. Not that he blamed his partner. He wouldn't mind following Bea to the shower, either.

"Nope, nope, nope." He shook his head and refilled his mug before heading to his own bathroom. "Don't even think about it, Shaw. Never going to happen."

He stripped off his clothes and stepped under the spray, not bothering to wait for the water to warm up. A cold shower was just the distraction he needed to keep from picturing Bea, naked and wet, a few feet down the hall.

So close, and yet so far away...

Was Bea as affected by him as he was by her?

Likely not, Micah decided, shaking his head as he toweled off. She might feel a twinge of nostalgia for the relationship they'd shared, but he doubted she still experienced any kind of attraction to him. He'd realized a long time ago that just because he considered Bea the love of his life didn't mean she placed him in the same category.

He sighed and forced his thoughts in a different direction. After taking Bea to pick up her clothes and toiletries, they'd go to her shop. He was looking forward to seeing the crime scene again; he'd been so concerned about Bea last night, he'd only had time for a cursory glance. The evidence techs would be done with the place now, so he could poke around without fear of contaminating the scene. He made a mental note to ask the guys on the team if they'd checked nearby businesses for security-camera footage that captured the street. Bea's boutique didn't have any cameras, but maybe they would get lucky with someone else's system.

Micah dressed quickly, his mind still turning over the case. Why had the Groom Killer spared Bea's life? Was he or she getting sloppy, or had there simply not been enough time to take care of Bea before leaving the scene? Or was it possible the Groom Killer wasn't Bea's attacker, after all, and her assault was a random event not tied to Joey McBurn's murder?

The questions had plagued him all night, and he was determined to find the answers.

One way or another, he was going to get to the bottom of this.

* * *

Bea hesitated at the door to her shop, feeling suddenly nervous about going inside.

Don't be silly, she chided herself. *It's broad daylight, and both Micah and Chunk are here. The place has been locked since last night. There's no one lying in wait in there.*

Her brain knew it was the truth, but she still felt a spike of anxiety as she remembered the way the lights had suddenly gone out yesterday evening. Her heart fluttered in her chest, and her palms grew damp with sweat as she recalled that strangely familiar smell…

She reached up to touch the bandage on her forehead with a fingertip. The numbing medication had worn off long ago, and the wound ached. But in a weird way, she was grateful for the injury. If she hadn't bled so much, Chunk and Micah probably wouldn't have found her. She might still be lying on the floor of her stockroom, injured or perhaps even dead.

The thought made her shudder and she nearly turned around, ready to postpone this visit to her shop. They could come back later—no one would think less of her for taking a few days off in the wake of what had happened.

"Hey." Micah's voice was quiet next to her, and he placed his hand on her shoulder. His touch was warm and comforting, and Bea felt her muscles relax. "You okay?"

She nodded, not knowing what to say. It seemed

ridiculous to be so scared of a building in the bright light of day, and yet she couldn't control her reaction.

Micah seemed to understand. "Want to come back another time? We don't have to do this now."

"No, it's okay. I want to." It was the truth. It was important to do this today, to rip the bandage off and take stock of the damage, both to her store and to her sense of safety. If she didn't face her fears now, it would be all too easy to succumb to avoidance and denial, and Bea refused to live her life that way.

A wet tongue swiped across her hand, and she glanced down to see Chunk staring up at her with those big brown eyes. "Thanks, buddy," she said to him, leaning down to scratch behind one of his ears. The dog's encouragement settled her nerves, and gave her the push she needed to insert the key into the lock and open the door.

The first thing she noticed was the smell. A metallic odor hung in the air, making her think of pencil shavings. She wrinkled her nose. Hopefully she could air the place out before the scent permeated the fabric of the wedding dresses.

Micah noticed her reaction. "It's the fingerprint dusting powder," he explained. "It's got carbon in it."

She glanced around, looking for the source of the smell. There was a fine dusting of black powder on the inside of the door, and she saw the register and counter were similarly adorned. "Oh, my God," she whispered, her breath catching in her throat. If the dresses were stained with the stuff, she might as well close her business now. She couldn't survive a hit to her inventory like that, not in her current financial straits.

Most of the gowns hung in clear plastic bags for display, but the bags weren't sealed so that it would be easy to remove the dresses for women to try on. Bea was going to have to painstakingly examine every dress and place it in a zipped storage bag before she could clean the store. It was a daunting task, and her heart sank as she looked around. She would need more than a few hours each morning to get this done.

With a sigh, Bea started for the stockroom, intending to retrieve some of the storage bags so she could get started. But as she moved to the back of the store she was horrified to find the mess only got worse. Black fingerprint powder seemed to cover every flat surface, and there were mysterious dark spots on the carpeting. Some areas were taped off while some sported what looked to be chalk markings. As she moved fully into the stockroom, she caught a glimpse of a dark red stain on the floor, surrounded by a corona of bandage wrappers and other trash. *That's where they found me*, she realized. The EMTs hadn't taken the time to clean up the debris left behind when they'd treated her, adding to the general mess of the place.

Tears stung her eyes as she took in the magnitude of the job facing her. Bea didn't know the first thing about cleaning up a crime scene, but she couldn't very well leave things as they were.

She felt warmth at her side and realized Micah had come to stand next to her. He didn't touch her, but she drew comfort from his presence nonetheless. "I know it looks bad," he said quietly. "But once it's all cleaned up you won't even be able to tell there was such a mess here."

Bea nodded and blinked hard. "Any tips on how to clean?" She tried to sound light, but her voice was thick with emotion and she knew she hadn't fooled Micah.

"Yeah. Don't try to do it yourself. I know a company that specializes in this kind of thing. They do good work."

His answer made her stomach knot. "I, uh… I don't think I can afford that right now." Crime-scene cleanup was probably an expensive job, and she barely had enough to cover the bills as it was.

"Do you have insurance?"

His question surprised her. "Of course."

Micah nodded. "In my experience, your insurance will cover the expense of the cleanup. The company will bill them, and you probably won't ever hear about it again. Want me to call them?"

"Yes, please." A wave of relief washed over her, carrying away the feeling of helplessness that had weighed her down since seeing the condition of the store. Maybe it wouldn't take long to put things to right again, after all.

Micah retrieved his phone and moved a few steps away to make the call. Bea glanced around, looking for Chunk. The dog was usually by his master's side, but at the moment he was nowhere to be found.

"Chunk?" she called. Was he still in the store?

Surely he wouldn't push the door open and escape onto the street? The thought quickened her step and she moved out of the stockroom in search of the dog.

She called his name again and was rewarded with a yip. Following the sound, she found Chunk sitting in the open doorway of the fitting room. "There you are," she said. "I was wondering…" The words died in her throat as she made the mistake of looking inside the small room.

The once elegant fitting room had been transformed into a scene from a horror movie. Blood saturated the upholstery of the padded chair in the corner, and there was a matching stain on the carpet just in front of the chair. The entire room looked like it had been dusted with soot, and there were various markings on the walls, the small table and the floor.

Chunk nosed her hand, clearly proud of himself. Bea absently patted his head, unable to tear her gaze away from the dark, rust-colored stain on the formerly cream fabric of the chair. She'd never seen so much blood before. Had the killer brought Joey here after shooting him? Or had Joey run into the store, desperately searching for a place to hide from his murderer?

Terror gripped her as she imagined the man cowering in the corner, straining to hear the sound of footsteps, praying the killer would pass him by. Bea had always thought of the fitting room as a happy, hopeful place, where a woman first donned the wedding dress of her dreams. Now it reeked of fear and desperation, and she knew she'd never look at this room the same way again.

"There you are."

Micah's voice made her jump, and she let out a small squeal. "Whoa," he said, reaching out to steady her. "I'm sorry. I didn't mean to scare you."

Bea shook her head. "It's okay. I came to look for Chunk, and found him here…" She trailed off, glancing back at the carnage with a frown.

Micah turned her away from the room. "I'm sorry about that. I should have warned you he'd head for the scene."

"Because of the blood?"

He nodded. "Even when he's not officially working, he'll still respond to the scent. He's trained not to ignore that particular odor, and his sense of smell is very strong."

"There's certainly enough blood here. Even I can kind of smell it." She wrinkled her nose at the coppery tang in the air and shivered.

Micah pulled her away from the room and Chunk followed them back into the store. "I feel so bad for him," Bea said softly. "I can't imagine how frightened Joey must have been." She wrapped her arms around herself, unable to stop thinking about the poor man.

Micah hesitated, then drew her against his chest. Bea stiffened, surprised at the contact. Then she melted against him, relaxing into his strength as his arms circled her.

"If it makes you feel any better, we don't think

Joey was killed here." His voice was a low rumble in her ear, the sound just as soothing as his words.

"You don't?"

Micah's chin brushed her hair as he shook his head. "No. There's no bullet hole in the chair, and if he was shot here, there would be a lot more blood."

Bea shivered, wondering how that was possible. To her eye, it looked like gallons of blood had been spilled in the small room. But what did she know about such matters?

Micah's arms tightened around her. Bea reveled in the contact—she had missed this, missed feeling his body against hers. They had always fit so perfectly together, as if they were made for each other. She closed her eyes and breathed in his scent, trying not to seem too obvious about it. Part of her felt a little guilty about enjoying his embrace. He was only trying to comfort her, and she shouldn't read too much into the gesture. But it had been so long since she'd been held by a man, and no one had ever taken Micah's place.

After a moment he pulled back and studied her face. "Better?"

She nodded, feeling a little sad. Micah's embrace had made her nostalgic for what they'd once shared, but she knew better than to dwell on the past.

"Good." He dropped his arms, releasing her. "The cleaning crew will be here in about an hour. Is there anything we need to do to protect your dresses before they get started?"

His question brought her back to reality and she

pushed aside her emotions to focus on work. "Yes. I need to get the gowns into zippered storage bags so they won't get exposed to any chemicals."

"Let's get started." He said it without hesitation, clearly ready and willing to do whatever it took to help her. A swell of gratitude rose in Bea's chest at this demonstration of Micah's generosity. He'd always been so thoughtful, and it was nice to know that time hadn't changed that about him.

She led the way to the stockroom and began retrieving the heavy bags. Micah carried them out into the store in piles, and together they set about tucking the dresses inside.

"Some of these are pretty heavy," he remarked, his tone revealing his surprise.

Bea smiled. "Yeah, the beadwork and layers of fabric add to the weight. But that's the price you pay for beauty."

"I suppose," he remarked, zipping a bag closed. "But I've always preferred the simple, elegant look."

"Me, too," she murmured, recalling the gown she'd picked out for their wedding. A pang stabbed her heart as she pictured the simple ivory sheath with its rows of seed pearls along the neckline and hem. She'd fallen in love with the dress the moment she'd seen it, and had bought it on the spot. Even after Micah had called things off, she couldn't bear to part with the dress, and it still hung in her closet at home. She took it out every once in a while when she was feeling particularly maudlin. Despite the passage of time, it was still her dream gown.

But she knew she'd never wear it.

Even if Bea did get engaged, she couldn't very well marry another man in the dress she'd picked out for Micah. So she kept it tucked in her closet, a reminder of past love and the life she might have led if things had turned out differently.

They worked in silence, the quiet punctuated by Chunk's gentle snoring as the dog snoozed on a rug a few feet away. Bea wasn't aware of the passage of time until a loud knock on the door interrupted her work.

"That'll be the cleaning crew," Micah said, striding to the door.

Bea glanced around as he opened the door. The two of them had made good progress; there were only a few dresses left to wrap. Micah gestured for her to join him. "They have some paperwork for you to sign, authorizing them to start cleaning. I'll finish up with the gowns while you take care of this."

It didn't take long—she skimmed over the permission forms and scribbled her name at the bottom. She turned to find Micah carefully sliding the last dress into the bag. *We make a good team*, she thought wistfully. Did he feel the same way? Or was he simply trying to be nice by helping her?

It doesn't matter, she told herself. The important thing was that the dresses were protected and the cleaning crew could get started. She had to stop reading too much into Micah's actions, or she was going to drive herself crazy.

"Ready?" Micah stood by the door, Chunk at his

side. Sunlight streamed through the window, sparking off the copper strands in his auburn hair. With his imposing height, broad shoulders and piercing green eyes, Micah was an impressive sight.

How is he still single? Handsome and kind, with a great sense of humor, to boot, Micah was a catch by anyone's standards. Why hadn't some lucky woman snapped him up?

She added that question to the long list of things she wanted to know about Micah and moved to join him. One day she'd ask him about his life and his time in the army. And maybe she'd even work up the courage to ask why he'd ended things so abruptly.

But not today. Last night's attack had left her feeling fragile and vulnerable, and she didn't think her heart could take another blow.

Chapter 6

Micah led Bea to the station's break room and placed the bag holding their lunch on the table. "Go ahead and start eating," he told her. "I'm going to check in with the guys. It shouldn't take too long." He headed for the door, then turned back. "And don't let Chunk fool you. That sad-eyed look he gives is a lie. He doesn't get people food, no matter what he tries to tell you."

Bea nodded and glanced down at the dog, who had already parked himself at her feet and was gazing longingly at the table.

"Don't beg, Chunk," Micah admonished. "It's not dignified."

His partner didn't bother to acknowledge him, and Micah left the pair alone, hoping Bea would be strong enough to resist Chunk's charms. He walked over to Brayden's desk, noting the dark circles under his friend's eyes. Brayden's clothes were rumpled, and Micah noted he hadn't changed since last night. Had Brayden slept here? *Correction*, he thought to himself, eying the large cup of coffee on the desk. *Did Brayden stay up all night working?*

Echo, the yellow Lab partnered with Brayden, reclined on a large pad by the desk. He lifted his head and began to wag his tail as Micah approached. "Hey there, buddy," Micah said softly, leaning down to scratch the dog's ears. Echo sat up and looked pointedly at Micah's side, clearly searching for Chunk. "He's in the break room," Micah explained. Echo stood and stretched, then trotted off in search of his friend.

Micah smiled faintly, impressed as always by the intelligence of the dogs in the K-9 unit. When he'd first joined the Rangers and had been partnered with Duke, he'd felt self-conscious about talking to the dog like he was a person. But it hadn't taken long for Micah to realize how empathetic Duke was, and it had soon become clear the animal understood more than just the simple commands he'd been taught.

After a second, he heard Chunk's happy yip of greeting, followed by a startled "Oh!" from Bea. *I probably should have warned her*, he thought. But both Echo and Chunk were good-natured dogs who got along well together, and he didn't think they'd cause any trouble.

Brayden looked up and ran his hand through his

already messy hair. "Hey," he said shortly. "Didn't think you'd make it in today."

"We had to stop by Bea's house and get some personal stuff, and then we went to the boutique. The place is a mess but I've got a cleaning crew there now. Hopefully they'll be finished by the end of the day."

Brayden nodded. "The evidence team finished up around three in the morning. Body's at the morgue, scheduled for an autopsy. The county coroner said he should be able to get to it today."

"And I take it the lab knows this case is a priority?"

"They do, but they also informed me they have a backlog of other priority cases to deal with first. So who knows how long it will take before we hear anything?"

Micah frowned, but he knew there was nothing to be done. The men and women who handled the forensic side of his investigations were a dedicated bunch, and he knew they weren't stalling on purpose. It was simply a supply-and-demand issue—there was a high demand for their services throughout the region and not enough of them to go around.

"Maybe I can help grease the wheels a bit," he muttered. He knew from experience that a catered lunch and a friendly smile went a long way in convincing the techs to put in a little overtime. In any event, it wouldn't hurt to build a little goodwill with the crew.

Carson and Shane wandered over, and Brayden nodded at the pair. "Any good news?" Micah asked. "Please tell me your neighborhood canvass turned up a witness to Tucker Frane's murder?"

"Nope." Carson grinned. "That would be too easy."

"And ballistics aren't back yet?"

Shane shook his head. "Owen's out sick today, so it hasn't been processed yet."

Frustration filled Micah. "He's sick?" he repeated incredulously. Now was a hell of a time for the ballistics tech to miss work, and Micah briefly considered driving to the man's house and bringing him in so they could get some answers.

"Afraid so," Shane said. "His supervisor said he had a nasty case of the flu. Even had to go to the ER for rehydration."

"Oh." Micah's irritation vanished, replaced with sympathy for the young man. "That's rough."

Finn walked over to the group, a file folder in his hand. "Oh good, you're all here. Saves me some time."

"What's up, chief?" Micah asked.

"Time for an impromptu meeting." Finn raised his voice to be heard over the din of the room. "Heads-up, ladies and gentlemen. Gather round, please."

Chairs scraped against the linoleum and feet shuffled as people stopped their work and walked over. Finn waited until the group had assembled, then nodded his head. "We've just had a report from the local FBI office regarding Demi Colton."

A murmur rippled through the crowd, and Micah's interest sharpened. Did they have another lead?

"An FBI agent reports spotting Demi in Walker's Creek yesterday evening around six."

Micah frowned. "That's, what? About sixty miles to the east?"

Finn nodded. "Yes. He says she's changed her hair—it's now short and blond."

"Whoa, wait a minute," Carson interjected. "We have a witness for my brother's murder who described Demi's long, curly red hair."

"And yesterday's witness described her long, curly hair, as well," Micah said. "Tucker Frane said her hair had been dyed brown, but it was still the same style."

Finn held up a hand. "I hear what you're saying, guys. I'm just telling you what the agent says he saw."

Micah crossed his arms over his chest, his skepticism mounting. "I don't suppose the agent got a closer look?"

Finn shook his head. "No. He lost her in a crowd."

"Of course," Micah muttered.

"There's more," Finn reported. "The agent said he's sure she's pregnant."

Another murmur started up, and Micah saw a few of his fellow officers nodding. They'd suspected Demi was pregnant, and had even found a discarded positive pregnancy test hidden in Demi's home during an earlier search.

The fact that the FBI agent had spotted a pregnant woman matching Demi's description was compelling, Micah had to admit. It wasn't hard to change a hairstyle, so it was possible Demi really was blonde now. But Micah still had a hard time believing she was in Walker's Creek.

"There's our motive," said Lucas Gage. He was a bounty hunter who contracted with the Red Ridge police department, and he and Demi were professional rivals of a sort. "Demi snapped when she discovered she's pregnant. She started this killing spree to get back at Bo for moving on with his life."

It was a compelling motive. Demi and Bo Gage, victim number one, had been a couple before he'd dumped her for Hayley Patton. Bo had been killed the night before his wedding. But Micah wasn't so sure Demi was guilty. Some evidence pointed to her, yes, but some of the pieces just didn't add up...

"No way," said Shane. "Bo hasn't been the only victim. Why continue to kill if Demi only wanted revenge on Bo?"

Lucas shrugged. "Like I said, she snapped."

Brayden spoke up, his voice tight with emotion. "You're forgetting something. It's not just grooms who are dying now. We have a dead witness. That's not part of the Groom Killer's usual pattern."

"And serial killers don't suddenly change their behavior," Shane added.

The room fell silent as the officers considered these new facts. Micah frowned as his thoughts swirled. Something the chief had said was bothering him, but he couldn't quite put his finger on what...

Suddenly, lightning struck. "Chief?" he asked. "What time did the FBI agent say he'd spotted Demi in Walker's Creek?"

Finn glanced back at the file in his hands. "Six in the evening."

Micah shook his head. "Impossible. Our witness from last night claims he saw her shoot Joey McBurn at six thirty in the alley. There's no way she could have made it to Red Ridge from Walker's Creek in half an hour."

Brayden nodded in agreement, and Micah could tell his friend's belief in his sister's innocence was bolstered by the discrepancy. "Someone is wrong," Brayden said. "Either Tucker Frane was lying about what he saw last night, or the FBI agent is mistaken."

"And we all know which option you're rooting for," someone muttered.

Brayden's jaw clenched, but he didn't respond to the quiet taunt. Micah was proud of his friend for taking the high road—he knew how difficult this case was for him.

Was it Demi the FBI agent had seen? Or was it simply someone who resembled her with different hair? If the FBI agent had seen a decoy, had Frane been killed for telling the truth about seeing Demi?

Finn's gaze sharpened on the gathering. "That's enough," he said firmly. "You all have jobs to do. Stay alert and focused, and think outside the box. The clues to solving these murders are in front of us. We just have to put them together in the right way."

He waved his hands, dismissing the group. As everyone wandered back to their desks, Micah saw Bea standing in the doorway of the break room, holding the brown paper sack that contained his lunch. She walked over, Chunk and Echo at her heels.

Micah had to smile at the sight. She looked like an angelic Pied Piper with her canine entourage. Both dogs gazed up at her adoringly, and Micah had a sneaking suspicion Bea hadn't been able to resist sharing her food with them.

"Did you finish eating?"

She nodded and handed the bag to him. "I thought you might want your burger before it gets too cold."

"Thanks." He took the bag and led her to his desk, a few feet away. He gestured for her to take the empty chair in front of his station, and Chunk pawed at his bed, walking in a counterclockwise circle three times before settling in for a nap. "Please tell me you didn't give him too much food."

Bea glanced at the dog and smiled. "Oh, no. He didn't get any of my burger. But I did find a jar of treats in the cupboard…" She trailed off, and Micah chuckled.

"Uh-huh. Did you find them on your own, or did you have help?"

Her cheeks flushed a pretty pink. "Well, the other dog did give me a little guidance."

"I'm sure he did," Micah replied.

"Echo," Brayden admonished, his tone one of affectionate exasperation. Echo's tail thumped against the floor, the dog clearly unrepentant about his actions. "I'm sorry about that. He thinks with his stomach."

"It's okay," Bea replied. "He probably figured I'm an easy mark."

Brayden turned back to his work, and Micah unwrapped his burger. It was a little on the cold side, but it was food and he was hungry.

Bea scooted closer to his desk and leaned in, as if

she had a confession. The neckline of her shirt gaped open, exposing the tops of her breasts. Micah's mouth went dry at the sight, and he quickly forced his eyes back up to her face. He swallowed hard and reached for a stale cup of coffee to wash down the burger before he choked.

"I heard what you all were talking about," she said softly. "About Demi being spotted in Walker's Creek yesterday evening."

Micah dabbed at his mouth with a paper napkin and nodded, not trusting his voice. He hadn't meant for Bea to learn so much about the investigation, but he also knew she wasn't like her father. Bea could keep a secret, and she wouldn't go blabbing to the press about what she knew.

"I know my opinion probably doesn't mean much, but I don't think Demi is the one who attacked me last night."

"Oh? Why is that?" Was Bea simply being loyal to her cousin, or was there a compelling reason she thought Demi was innocent?

Bea shook her head. "I can't quite explain it, but I know it wasn't her. I'm pretty sure it was a woman who hit me, because of the perfume. I recognize it from somewhere, but I just don't know where. What I am certain of is that Demi has never worn perfume like that in her life, and I can't imagine she'd start now."

Micah studied Bea's face, sympathy welling in his chest. "It's possible she's trying to disguise herself by changing her hair and clothes. Adding a distinctive perfume that she only wore last night would further confuse any potential witnesses."

Bea considered that for a moment. "But someone said your witness from last night is dead. Why go to the trouble of killing that man, but leave me alive?"

It was the question that had been bothering Micah ever since he'd found her on the floor of her boutique. "I don't know," he admitted. "Maybe she heard Chunk bark and realized the police were close. She had to get away before we came in."

Bea shook her head. "It doesn't take that long to shoot someone," she said matter-of-factly.

A chill raced through his limbs at the reminder. Bea was right. It was the work of a second to pull a trigger, a twitch of muscle, really. A small, insignificant movement that had profound consequences, as he'd learned all too well during his time in both the Army Rangers and on the police force.

He steered his thoughts away from the desert and back to the present. "Maybe she panicked," he offered. "Or maybe she got cold feet at the idea of killing her cousin."

Bea lifted one shoulder in a shrug. "Maybe. But to be honest, we've never been that close. If she had no problem killing Bo, the man she loved, I doubt she'd have an issue shooting me."

"You didn't break her heart and leave her pregnant," Micah pointed out. "Hell hath no fury, as I'm sure you know."

The strangest expression crossed Bea's face, and

for a second, he thought she was going to either burst into tears or start laughing.

"Yes, I've heard that line before," she said dryly. She leaned back and studied him as he finished his burger. "Look, I know I'm not giving you much to go on here, but I know in my bones the person who attacked me isn't Demi. And since I have a hard time believing my little boutique was the scene of so much illicit traffic last night, I think whoever killed Joey is the same person who hit me."

But that would rule out Demi as the Groom Killer. And he couldn't make that leap just yet. "Once we get the lab results back we'll have a better idea of how many people traipsed through the shop last night. But I tend to agree with you—the killer and your attacker are likely one and the same."

"And since I know it wasn't Demi, then she can't be the one who killed Joey or the other men." Bea's expression was triumphant, but Micah shook his head.

"That's taking it too far. I know you want Demi to be innocent, but there's quite a bit of evidence against her at this point."

Bea's face fell, and Micah kicked himself for having to disappoint her. But he couldn't let her get her hopes up when it was likely her cousin was guilty of at least one murder, if not all four. Three grooms, killed the night before their wedding, black cummerbunds stuffed into their mouths. The MO had been the same in all three murders. Only the fourth murder, Tucker Frane's, was different—no cummerbund—but he wasn't a groom. Just a witness.

He knew the Coltons didn't want to believe one of their own was responsible for such heinous acts. Still, it was a possibility that couldn't be ignored, and Bea and the rest of her family needed to start coming to terms with the fact that practically anyone was capable of committing murder, if pushed too far.

But were last night's killings really the work of the Groom Killer? Or had someone wanted Joey McBurn dead and decided to stage the scene to lead the police down the wrong path? The idea seemed a bit far-fetched, but Micah had to admit it was a possibility. Hopefully the forensic results would shed more light on the case and help him figure out which questions to focus on and which were nothing more than speculation.

He wiped his mouth and tossed the empty wrapper and bag into the trash can by his desk. "I need you to do something for me, please."

Bea nodded at once, causing a tendril of blond hair to fall in front of one eye. Micah's fingers itched to brush it back, but he fought the urge to touch her. Bea likely wouldn't welcome the gesture, and if any of the other officers saw he'd never hear the end of it.

He had to keep things professional between them, now more than ever. If his fellow squad members thought he was getting personally involved with Bea Colton, they might doubt his impartiality and ability to work on the Groom Killer case. It was difficult enough having so many of Demi Colton's relatives on the force—the last thing Micah wanted was for his judgment to be called into question because of his personal life.

"What do you need from me?" Bea's voice broke into his thoughts and he focused on her face again. Her expression was a mixture of interest and determination, and Micah realized she wanted to help him. It was clear she wouldn't be content to bring a book and read while he worked in the afternoons, so he was going to have to figure out a way to safely incorporate her into his activities.

Micah pulled a notepad and pen from a desk drawer. "I know I asked you questions last night in the hospital, but I don't have an official statement from you yet. I'd like you to write down everything you remember from last night, starting from the time you began to close up the shop. No detail is too insignificant, so please include everything. And if something strange happened earlier in the day, write that down, too."

"Okay." Bea took the pen and pad from him and glanced around. "Is there someplace I can sit so I'm out of the way? A spare office, maybe?"

Micah stood. "I'll unlock a room for you. It'll be quiet in there, so you can focus." He led her down a hall to one of the interrogation rooms, located at the back of the building. "The bathroom is farther down this hall on your right, and you know where the break room is. Feel free to help yourself to coffee or soda while you work."

Bea took a seat and placed the pad of paper in

front of herself. "This might take me a while," she said doubtfully. "Will that be a problem for you?"

"Not at all," he assured her. "Take your time. I don't want you to feel rushed at all. I'll keep myself busy while you take care of this, and when you're done we'll go back and check on the boutique." The cleaning crew had told him it would only take one day to finish the job. He and Bea could swing by on the way home to make sure everything looked good before she reopened the store tomorrow morning.

He left her to it and headed to the break room, needing something to drink before he got back to work. He felt unsettled and a little antsy, and it wasn't just Bea's presence that had him off-balance.

Something about Joey McBurn's death and the attack on Bea didn't add up. Micah felt like there was a key piece of information staring him in the face, but he wasn't recognizing it for what it was.

The chief's words echoed in his mind: *The clues to solving these murders are in front of us. We just have to put them together in the right way.*

It was that simple and that complicated.

"I can't believe it." Bea turned in a slow circle, staring wide-eyed at the boutique. "It looks completely normal!"

Micah smiled at her reaction. "I told you these guys were good."

"You did. But I never thought they'd be magicians." She walked over to the fitting room and shook her head. "The carpet looks brand-new."

Micah joined her, peering over her shoulder. The small room was completely transformed, and if he hadn't seen the state of things beforehand, even he would have had trouble believing they were looking at what had recently been a crime scene.

"I wonder what happened to the chair?"

"Probably too tough to adequately clean without ruining it," Micah commented. "I know you can't tell, but they ripped up the carpet and cleaned the padding and the floor underneath, as well. They likely would have had to rip open the chair to clean the stuffing inside, and that's not an easy repair."

"Well, it's a small price to pay," Bea said.

He smiled, pleased that she was happy with the results. She'd been so upset this morning about the state of her shop, he was glad the company he'd recommended had done a good job in restoring things to their usual state. He knew from talking to other crime victims that a swift return to normal helped them recover from the trauma they'd experienced.

"Do we need to take care of anything before you close up for the night?"

Bea shook her head. "No. I'll start unwrapping the dresses tomorrow morning. It will give me something to do between customers."

"Fair enough. Any thoughts on what you'd like to do for dinner tonight?"

She wrinkled her nose. "No fast food, please."

"Ah, okay." His thoughts raced as he tried to come up with another option. He didn't have much in the way of groceries at home, and he doubted Bea was in the mood for a TV dinner. Red Ridge had several decent restaurants, but he didn't want to go anywhere too fancy…

"Can we stop at the store? I'll get a few things and whip up something for us."

It was on the tip of Micah's tongue to refuse. He didn't want her to get into the habit of cooking for him, and having her in his kitchen was a little too domestic for his liking. Still, it was a better option than eating out, and she really didn't seem to mind…

"All right," he decided. "But I'm buying the groceries."

"We'll split the cost," Bea answered. "After all, I'm eating the food, too."

Knowing he wasn't going to win this one, Micah nodded and held the door open for Bea. She stopped to lock the boutique for the night, and a breeze caught her hair, sending the strands dancing. He caught a whiff of his shampoo, and a wave of possessiveness surged through him.

Mine.

The word popped into his head without warning, a roaring claim that startled him with its intensity. Something about smelling his soap on Bea's body short-circuited his brain and made him respond like a caveman. Fortunately, his self-control kicked in and stopped him from tossing her over his shoulder and striding off into the sunset in search of privacy and a flat surface.

No, not mine, he thought firmly. *Not anymore.*

"Ready?" Her hazel eyes stared up at him, her gaze

open and trusting. She had no idea how she affected him, and he was going to do everything in his power to keep it that way. If Bea knew Micah still had feelings for her she'd regard him with pity, and his pride couldn't take that blow.

He cleared his throat, forcing the unexpected wave of emotion back into its box and slamming the lid closed. "After you."

Chapter 7

"This is amazing."

Micah forked another bite of pasta into his mouth, then leaned back and closed his eyes, his expression blissful.

Bea smiled, pleased at his obvious enjoyment of the meal. "I'm glad you like it." Spaghetti carbonara was one of her go-to quick meals, and she'd made a simple tossed salad to accompany the pasta. It wasn't a fancy dinner, by any standards, but Micah's reaction made her think he didn't cook for himself very often.

"Where did you learn how to cook like this?" he asked between bites. "When I had dinner with your family all those years ago, your father had a personal chef."

Bea's smile slipped as she recalled that evening

and her father's behavior. She'd invited Micah to dinner, wanting him to meet her father and siblings. Her sisters had been friendly, if a bit indifferent, toward Micah, but Fenwick had been downright nasty. He'd made it clear that Micah was not welcome and that he wasn't good enough for Fenwick's daughter. To his credit, Micah hadn't argued or tried to defend himself, and to her shame, Bea hadn't been able to stand up to her father. Micah had left immediately after dinner, and Bea had retreated to her room, too upset to speak to anyone.

"My grandmother taught me," she said, shifting her thoughts in a more pleasant direction. "She made it a point to teach me basic life skills, because she knew I'd eventually move out of my father's house. She always said she didn't want me to grow up to be one of those useless people who don't know how to fix a meal or sew on a button."

Micah smiled. "Sounds practical."

Bea nodded. "Oh, yes. She also taught me everything I know about the boutique. I used to spend a lot of time there when I was a child, and I think that's why she left me the store in her will."

"She knew you'd take care of it."

"That's true, but I think there was more to it." Bea wiped her mouth with a napkin and took a sip of water. "I think she wanted to give me a way out, a means of independence from my father. He didn't want me to take over the business, but I insisted. And I think Gram knew I would. She gave me a way to support myself, so I wouldn't be under my father's thumb my whole life."

Micah tilted his head to the side, studying her as he finished eating. "I think you would have made your own way, regardless," he said thoughtfully. "You've always been independent."

Bea's cheeks warmed at the compliment. She'd worked hard to distance herself from her overbearing father, but thinking about her relationship with Micah made her wish she'd pushed back a little harder while they'd been dating. Would things have been different if she had done a better job of defending Micah, of calling her father out on his rude behavior in the moment, instead of waiting until they were alone?

"I owe you an apology," she said, taking a deep breath. Maybe it was silly of her to bring up the past, but Micah deserved to know she hadn't forgotten the way he'd been treated and that she didn't agree with it. She couldn't change what had happened, but she could let him know she was ashamed of her father's behavior and her failure to act.

His eyebrows shot up and his green eyes went wide. "Oh?" He shifted a little in his chair, looking wary.

Bea nodded. "Yes. I'm sorry for the way my father treated you when we were dating. And I'm sorry I wasn't brave enough to stand up to him when he was being so horrible to you."

Micah's shoulders relaxed and he shook his head. "Don't worry about it. You're not responsible for your father's actions."

"I know, but I should have defended you more, instead of arguing with him when we were alone."

"We were kids." He shrugged and gave her a half smile. "Besides, you and I both know your dad wouldn't have tolerated that kind of insubordination. If you had given him a hard time about his behavior, he probably would have cut you off."

Bea considered his words, knowing he was right. But would that have been so bad? She entertained a brief fantasy of what it would have been like to live with Gram, working in the shop and spending time with Micah free from the heavy weight of her father's disapproval.

It was a nice thought, but she realized it wouldn't have been fair to her grandmother to ask her to step in like that. And there was no sense in dwelling on what might have been, no matter how much Bea wished things had turned out differently.

Micah's voice broke into her thoughts. "Don't let your dad's actions bother you. I stopped thinking about it a long time ago."

Sensing he was done talking about the issue, Bea nodded and pushed back from the table. She gathered up dishes and walked over to the sink. A second later, Micah's arm slid around her side as he placed his own dishes on the counter. She jumped a bit, startled, and turned to find him standing close. He leaned forward and her heart flip-flopped in her chest. Was he going to kiss her? Her muscles tensed and her lips parted in anticipation.

Micah reached around her and turned the water

on, then leaned back. "I'll take care of the dishes," he said.

"Oh." Disappointment flooded Bea's system, followed quickly by embarrassment. Of course Micah wasn't going to kiss her. It was foolish of her to think otherwise. Her cheeks heated and she glanced down, hoping Micah didn't notice her reaction.

"Let me get out of your way," she murmured. He angled his body so she could slide past. Bea flattened herself along the counter, careful not to touch him as she moved away from the sink. She returned to the table, clearing the rest of the dishes for Micah. Then she stood in the kitchen, feeling useless as she watched him work.

The light over the sink made the copper strands in his hair glow. It was a little longer than she remembered him wearing it, the ends curling at the nape of his neck and over the tips of his ears. Micah had always kept his hair short, even before joining the military. This more casual look was likely a testament to his busy schedule rather than a sign he was embracing a new style.

"You need a haircut," she said, speaking without thought.

He sighed, his shoulders shifting under the fabric of his shirt as he scrubbed a pot. "I know. I just haven't had time. I might just shave my head and be done with it."

"No!" Bea took a step forward, dismayed at the thought of Micah losing his beautiful red hair.

He cast a glance over his shoulder, apparently picking up on the distress in her voice. "I've had it shaved before, when I was in the army. It took a few days for me to get used to it, but it was a lot more convenient than what I'm dealing with now. I was one of the lucky ones, too. My head doesn't have a funny shape to it, like some of the other guys."

"Please don't do that," she said. He shrugged, as if he didn't care one way or another. Bea struggled to find something persuasive to say that wouldn't make her sound like a crazy person. How could she explain that she'd always loved his hair without revealing that she still had feelings for him? Micah was no fool. If she was too insistent, he'd want to know why she cared so much. And that wasn't a question she could simply ignore. She had a terrible poker face, and Micah knew it. If he asked her a question like that, her expression would tell him everything he wanted to know before she could even open her mouth to speak.

"I could trim the ends for you. Until you can get a real haircut."

Micah shut off the water and reached for a towel. He turned to face her, drying his hands as he moved. "Really?" He sounded curious, as if he was seriously contemplating her offer. Bea felt a momentary panic—what did she know about trimming hair?— but pushed it aside, nodding in what she hoped was a confident manner.

"You really wouldn't mind?"

"Not at all. It'll only take a minute." *I think.* She was quickly moving out of her depth, but how hard could it be to trim the ends of his hair? Bea had watched her stylist in the mirror during her own cuts, and it didn't look all that complicated.

"That would be great. It's been bugging me to have it so long."

"I can take care of it now, if you want. Do you have a pair of scissors I can use?"

Micah nodded. "I'll be right back." He walked out of the kitchen, and Bea sagged against the counter.

"What are you *thinking*?" she muttered to herself. She didn't know the first thing about giving a man a haircut. More importantly though, she was now going to have to touch Micah. To run her hands through his hair, to lean in close and smell his scent as she worked.

Idiot. Why couldn't she have just kept her mouth shut and let him do what he wanted? It probably would have been better for her in the long run if he *had* shaved his head—she'd always loved his hair, and if it was gone, maybe her attraction would wane.

"Probably not, though," she whispered. Micah was the total package, and her love for him wasn't conditional upon a single feature.

She heard him rummaging through drawers, likely in search of the scissors. No backing out now. She was going to have to do this. Did she have time to search for a quick tutorial online? Bea reached for her phone, but the sound of Micah's footsteps grew louder as he approached.

Okay, she thought, taking a deep breath. *This isn't*

*rocket science. And the nice thing about hair is that
it grows back.*

Micah appeared in the doorway, a towel slung over
his shoulders and a pair of scissors in his hand. "I was
thinking the back porch would be best. That way we
don't have any cleanup."

Bea smiled and nodded, as if this was her usual
arrangement. She followed him outside into the cool
night air and waited while he sat on a chair and ar-
ranged the towel around himself like a short cape.
The porch light cast everything in a sulfurous yellow
glow, making the moment seem even more surreal.

She took the scissors from him, then reached out
and ran her fingertips through the hair on the back
of his head, combing it over the edge of the towel. It
was just as soft as she remembered. A sigh rose in
the back of her throat but she bit her bottom lip before it could escape.

After a moment's hesitation, she began to cut.
Small, uncertain snips at first that barely took anything off. Then she grew bolder, daring to actually cut
into the length. One curled wisp fell to the ground,
followed quickly by another. The job grew easier as
she worked, the tension in her muscles draining away
as she realized she'd have to really try to mess things
up.

Her focus began to drift as she ran her fingers
through his hair. Memories of their time together
washed over her, making her melt inside. Even though
there was nothing sexual about this situation, Bea felt
a little thrill at the knowledge that a physically pow-

erful man was submitting to her touch. Micah had always been bigger and stronger, but his time in the military had turned his body into a lean, hard instrument. She'd felt the solid muscle of his chest pressed against her curves when he'd held her earlier, and the memory heated her blood. Too bad she wouldn't get to see the changes in his body for herself.

"How's it going?" His deep voice held a note of curiosity but not concern. He trusted her, and the knowledge was both humbling and exciting.

"Almost done," she replied. Bea could spend all night lingering with her hands on him, but she knew she needed to wrap things up before he grew suspicious. Normal haircuts didn't take long, and she was only giving him a trim. He probably wouldn't appreciate the extra attention, especially from her.

As if on cue, a pang of longing speared her heart. She pushed it aside and focused on her hands again. *Finish the job*, she told herself. And if she happened to run her fingers through his hair more than was strictly necessary? Hopefully he wouldn't notice.

She brushed at his shoulders, gathering more sense memories she could take out and examine later, once she was alone. Knowing she couldn't stall any longer, she gathered the ends of the towel and flung it away from him, shaking the loose hair into the yard.

"All done," she said, hoping he wouldn't detect the note of disappointment in her voice.

No such luck. "You okay?"

She turned to find him standing, his large hands

brushing at his hair and shoulders. Bea offered him a smile. "Yeah. Just hoping you like your new cut."

Micah touched the tips of his ears, then the back of his neck. "Feels good to me." He smiled warmly and, after a second's hesitation, stepped forward and gave her a gentle hug.

Bea closed her eyes as his arms wrapped around her. Time seemed to stop as she soaked up the feel of him, his scent and warmth enveloping her in a familiar, comforting embrace. She knew he meant to keep the hug impersonal and friendly, but her body didn't care. Heat suffused her limbs until she thought she might melt against him.

He pulled away, leaving her cold. Tears stung her eyes and she looked down, blinking hard so Micah wouldn't notice. She felt him studying her, probably wondering why she was acting so strangely.

"It's my bedtime," she announced with false cheer. She tried to step around his big body, but Micah held out an arm, blocking her path to the door.

"Why do I get the feeling you're upset about something?"

She tried to wave away his concern, but he wasn't having it. "Are you worried about your store? Or about the case? I promise, we'll get to the bottom of this soon."

Bea seized on the excuse and nodded vigorously. "I just hope none of the dresses were ruined during the cleaning process. I'm sure they're all fine, but I'll feel better once I examine everything tomorrow morning."

Micah dropped his arm, but she could see the glint of skepticism in his green eyes and knew he didn't really believe her. Still, he didn't block her as she moved toward the door.

"You've always been a bad liar, Bea." His voice was soft, less of a challenge and more of an observation. She spun around to face him, anger building in her chest as she stared at his back. How dare he question her? He'd given up all claim on her secrets when he'd sent that letter, breaking her heart into a million tiny pieces. And now he wanted to pretend he cared about what was bothering her?

Fine, she thought darkly. *You asked for it.*

"You want to know what's wrong?" Her throat was tight with emotion, but she forced the words out.

Micah turned to face her, his expression unreadable. "I asked, didn't I?" His voice was even, as if he was trying to control his temper. His oh-so-reasonable tone only fueled her agitation, making her even more reckless.

"Here you go, then. I've missed you. I still miss you. How do you like that?" She threw her arms out to the side and took a little bow. It felt *good* to finally say the words out loud, to truly acknowledge her emotions. She didn't know what was going to happen now, but it was nice to cast off the burden of pretending that she was unaffected by his presence.

Micah froze, his big body going stiff before her eyes. Bea shook her head and laughed. The sound was harsh in the night air, and for a second, the crickets stopped chirping their evening song. "Not what you were expecting to hear, was it?"

A kaleidoscope of emotions paraded across Micah's face: shock, disbelief and something that might have been joy. Bea waited a moment, wanting to hear his response. When it became clear he didn't have anything to say, she walked past him toward the door. Her stomach churned, her anger quickly morphing into embarrassment. *Way to go*, she thought. Once again, she'd opened herself up to Micah, handing him another opportunity to hurt her. *When will you learn?*

He didn't try to stop her as she breezed by. But just as her hand landed on the doorknob, his voice cut through the silence.

"I've missed you, too."

She lost her grip on the knob and turned slowly, hardly daring to believe her ears. "What?" Had he really just said that, or had her brain simply conjured up the words she most wanted to hear?

Micah shot her an angry glare, his green eyes alight with temper. "You heard me."

Bea's heart rate kicked up a notch as she watched him stalk closer. His body practically vibrated with emotion, making him seem somehow bigger than usual. He eyed her up and down, like a predator searching for weakness in its chosen prey. But Bea wasn't afraid. Anticipation flared in her belly, sending a tingling sensation through her limbs. The fine hairs on her arms and neck rose to attention, and her skin felt hypersensitive, as if the lightest kiss of air would cause her body to ignite.

"I missed you every day while I was at boot camp. Every night in that godforsaken desert. And all the hours in between." The words were clipped and tight, verbal knives he threw at her with abandon. He stopped when his body was inches from hers, and Bea felt the heat pouring off him.

"I thought I'd eventually forget you. But I didn't." She heard a note of disappointment in his voice, an echo of her own regret for never getting over him.

"And now, after all these years, here you are. A part my life again."

Bea bristled at the implied accusation that she had somehow orchestrated their reunion. "I didn't ask to be attacked," she said icily. "I didn't ask for you and your dog to find me."

"No, you didn't," he murmured. "You just turned those wide hazel eyes on me and acted like I was some kind of savior. Like I was the only one who could keep you safe."

"I'm only human, Micah," she snapped. "I saw you when my guard was down. I let my emotions take over."

He nodded and leaned forward. "Now it's my turn."

Before Bea could even blink, Micah cupped her face in his hands and lowered his mouth to hers.

Chapter 8

What are you doing?

The thought popped into Micah's head as soon as his lips met Bea's, but he ignored the question. He was operating on pure emotion; reason held no sway over him now.

Bea's admission had shocked him. Never in a million years had he expected to hear that she missed him. Joy had flooded his system as her words had sunk in, followed quickly by anger. How dare she say that, after all this time? She'd made her choice years ago—was he supposed to feel grateful that she had somehow changed her mind and wanted him again?

Her expression had given him no clue as to what she'd expected him to say. Truth be told, she didn't appear happy. Bea hadn't acted like a woman who was eager for a reunion, all coy glances and blushing smiles. If anything, she had hurled the words at him, as if she blamed him for her emotions.

Like this was his fault.

He hadn't been the one to break things off. And if she thought that her little confession was going to send him into paroxysms of gratitude, she was mistaken. Micah wasn't going to simply fall at her feet. *If* he decided to give her another chance, it was going to be on his terms.

The kiss was punishing, more of a reclaiming than a reunion. Micah poured all of his emotions into the connection, his frustration, anger and confusion making him feel a little desperate, a little reckless. He nipped at Bea's lips with his teeth—not so hard as to hurt her, but rough enough to make it clear this was not going to be an uncomplicated reconciliation.

In the dim recesses of his brain, a muted alarm sounded.

Dial it back. It's too much, too soon.

Micah's self-control began to reboot, and he relaxed a bit. Despite his intense emotions, he didn't want to frighten Bea.

He needn't have worried. She gave as good as she got, kissing him back with a ferocity to match his own.

One hand gripped his biceps, squeezing tightly as she tangled her tongue with his. Her other hand roamed across his chest, her fingers digging into his muscles. The fabric of his shirt muted the scratch of her nails, but the sensation was enough to ignite a fire of need in his lower belly.

He backed her up against the door, ignoring Chunk's startled *woof!* from inside the house. He slipped his hands under Bea's arms and lifted her body, putting their mouths into better alignment. She locked her legs around his waist and gripped his shoulders, a low moan emerging from deep in her throat.

The sound cut through the fog of his arousal and Micah snapped back to reality, his head clearing in an instant. His body clamored for more—more contact, more access to Bea's soft skin and her intoxicating smell. It had been ages since he'd held a woman in his arms, longer still since he'd been with Bea. It would be so easy to forget about the past and live in the moment, to take her inside and slake his lust until they were both tired and sweaty and spent.

Certain parts of his body rejoiced at the thought, but his heart wasn't on board with that plan. As much as he wanted Bea, and he *did* want her—his need for her was so great it was almost painful—he couldn't take her into his bed until he knew he could trust her. He'd tried before to keep his emotions out of the bedroom, but he wasn't that kind of man. He needed to feel an emotional and intellectual connection to a woman before he seduced her, and he couldn't simply dismiss all the unfinished business between himself and Bea just so he could scratch a physical itch.

He pulled away slowly, easing out of the kiss. Bea

looked up at him with a question in her eyes, her lips swollen and parted.

"I'm sorry," he said, his voice rough. "I shouldn't have done that. I, uh…" He shook his head and took a deep breath, searching for the right words. "I just need some time to think."

Bea's expression cleared and she nodded. Micah watched as her guard snapped back into place, transforming her from the passionate woman of a moment ago into a polite stranger once again. "That's a good idea. For both of us."

She unhooked her ankles and he gently lowered her until her feet hit the ground. He stepped back, putting more space between them. The gesture was for his benefit as much as hers. Despite his logical words, his body still pulsed with heat and desire. If he didn't get away from her soon he was liable to do something stupid, like kiss her again.

Bea ran her hand down the front of her shirt, smoothing the fabric back into place. She glanced up at him, looking uncertain. "I, uh, I think I'll go to bed now," she said.

Micah heard the tremor in her voice, and a selfish part of him was happy to know he wasn't the only one shaken by their kiss. "Yeah," he replied lamely. "It's getting late."

She nodded. "Good night." With that, she turned and bolted through the door, back into the safety of the house.

Micah hung back, wanting to give her a minute so she wouldn't feel like he was chasing her. He watched through the glass as she stopped to pet Chunk. The dog nosed her hand in greeting, then got to his feet and trotted off after her as she walked down the hall. He waited a few more seconds, giving her time to make it to the guest bedroom and shut the door. Then he stepped inside, flipping the lock behind him with a sigh.

He ran his hand through his hair, briefly surprised to find it so short. After a second he began to pace the length of the living room. He needed to move, needed to do something with all the excess energy in his body. Right now he felt unsettled and jumpy. The sensations were unfamiliar and unwelcome, and he knew until he found some way to deal with them he wasn't going to be able to sleep.

Moving quickly, he headed for his bedroom, keeping his gaze firmly away from the closed door to the guest room. He changed into shorts and a T-shirt and slipped into his running shoes, then headed for the door. He paused briefly on the porch, wondering if he should tell Bea where he was going. But no—she was settling in for the night, and he didn't want to see her right now. She should be safe while he was gone. No one aside from his fellow officers and her father knew she was staying with him, so if the killer wanted to tie up loose ends, they wouldn't know to look here. And Chunk was with her; despite the dog's laid-back disposition, he made a good guardian. Still, he would stay close to the house just in case. Satisfied the world would continue to turn while he took a personal moment, Micah locked the door and set off down the gravel drive.

I'm not running away, he asserted as his feet pounded against the uneven ground. *I'm just clearing my head.*

He set a punishing pace, relishing the burn and welcoming the sweat it brought. But after forty minutes of making a wide circle around the property, Micah was forced to admit his thoughts were still as jumbled as ever.

Had Bea really missed him? Or was this some kind of sick joke? He'd never known her to be deliberately cruel, but she had broken his heart in the most impersonal of ways.

Maybe she regretted it, though. Maybe now that she was older, she realized that the way she had ended things was wrong. Hell, maybe she had spent the intervening years searching for Mr. Right, only to realize she wouldn't ever be able to top what they'd had.

He snorted at the egotistical thought, but the possibility intrigued him. He certainly hadn't been able to find anyone to replace her. But if that was the case, if she wanted him back because she hadn't found anyone better, could he really be satisfied knowing she had merely settled for him?

No. The answer was automatic, as instinctive as his next breath. Whatever happened next between them, Micah had to know that Bea was in it for the right reasons.

If she even wanted him back.

All she had said was that she missed him. Micah

realized it was a bit of a leap to go from that simple statement to assuming she wanted a relationship again. Was he jumping to conclusions, projecting what he'd wanted to hear instead of listening to what she'd really meant?

He ran up the porch steps, his feet thumping loudly against the wooden boards. He grabbed the door handle, then thought better of it and began to stretch instead. The cool breeze felt good against his heated skin, and his muscles ached pleasantly as he bent and twisted, stretching his limbs.

His mind drifted, thoughts turning to the Groom Killer case. The sooner he and the rest of the team solved this mystery, the sooner Bea would go back to her place and he would have the space he needed to think. Why had the killer suddenly started targeting witnesses? Was that a one-time event or the beginning of a new pattern? He made a mental note to bring in the first witness, Paulie Gains, and question the man again. He was the one who'd said he saw Demi Colton running near the crime scene of the first murder. Maybe they should put him under surveillance, to see if the killer came back for—

The front door swung open with a loud bang, and Micah whirled to find Bea standing in the doorway, clutching a golf club. Her eyes were wide and her face was pale, but she looked determined despite her obvious fear.

"Oh. It's you." Her breath rushed out in a sigh, and her body visibly deflated.

Micah's heart retreated back into his chest. "Were you expecting someone else?"

Bea shook her head. "I wasn't sure. I heard thumps on the porch, and the doorknob rattled like someone was trying to get inside. You weren't here, so I grabbed the first thing I could find and thought I'd check it out."

"So you did." He couldn't decide if he was proud of her bravery or upset at her brash actions. If he'd been the Groom Killer or some other shady character, she could have been seriously hurt or worse. "Next time though, maybe you should just hide and dial 911."

She blushed and looked down, and he craned his neck to see over her shoulder. "Where's Chunk?"

"Asleep on the rug," she mumbled.

Micah bit back a smile. "Ah. Well, he's usually a pretty good judge of threats. If he's calm, you can be confident there's nothing to worry about."

"If you say so." She glanced up, her eyes traveling across his shoulders and down his stomach. Micah was suddenly aware of the way the sweat-soaked shirt clung to his body like a second skin. He plucked at the fabric and heard Bea's breath hitch in her throat. Her gaze took on a hungry, needy edge, triggering an answering response in Micah's body.

He cleared his throat, interrupting the moment before it turned into something neither one of them could ignore. "It's getting late. I should clean up and head to bed."

Bea blinked. "Yeah." She nodded mechanically

and turned, still clutching the golf club. "Good night," she said over her shoulder.

"Night." He followed her inside, his masculine pride pleased by her reaction to his body. Seeing her so flustered was a definite boost to his ego, and he chuckled softly as he made his way down the hall to his room. It was silly, but somehow the knowledge that Bea liked what she saw when she looked at him made him feel a little better about their situation.

Twenty minutes later, Micah climbed into bed feeling strangely content. Bea's words had left him with more questions than answers, but it seemed like they were at least moving forward in some way, instead of staying locked in the same superficial pattern of denial where they pretended not to have a shared past.

They still had a long way to go, but it was a step in the right direction.

Bea rubbed her eyes, stifling a yawn as she looked around the store. Everything was just as it had been before the attack; the gowns were out of the storage bags, the carpet was clean and every flat surface gleamed in the warm glow of the morning light streaming through the front windows of the shop. The place was picture-perfect, and Bea felt a moment's satisfaction at the thought that Gram would be proud.

Micah emerged from the back room. "All the bags are back in the plastic storage tubs. I took the liberty of putting the tubs on the shelves again. If you don't like them there, I'll be happy to move them."

"Thank you," Bea said, appreciating his help. "I'm sure they're fine where they are."

Micah nodded. "Do you think you'll be okay for a little bit? I've got some calls to make, and I thought I'd step out onto the sidewalk so you don't have to listen to me yammer."

Bea made a show of glancing around the empty boutique. "I think I can handle the crowd. Take your time." He nodded, and inspiration struck. "Would you mind picking up a coffee from the café on the corner while you're out there?"

Micah hesitated, but Bea pressed. "You can see the shop from the café. It'll be fine."

He nodded. "All right. Just a coffee, or do you want something fancy?"

"A big latte would be great."

Chunk lifted his head when he saw Micah heading for the door. Micah turned and spoke quietly to the dog. "Stay." Chunk settled his head on his paws with a contented sigh. "Remember," Micah said, aiming a wry smile in her direction. "As long as Chunk is calm, you have nothing to worry about."

Bea felt her cheeks warm at the reminder of her actions last night. "I'll keep that in mind."

The tinkling of the bell over the door announced Micah's departure. Bea sagged against the counter, relaxing for the first time that morning.

She hadn't slept well the night before. Her brain wouldn't turn off, replaying her conversation with Micah over and over again in an endless loop. She'd analyzed everything they'd said to each other, looking for hidden meanings or signs. But no matter how many times she relived those moments, she was left with a list of questions that both confused and intrigued her.

Micah seemed to still have feelings for her—his kiss was proof of that. Goose bumps broke out on her arms as Bea recalled the press of his solid strength against her chest, the feel of his hands on her face. His touch had been gentle despite the intensity of the kiss, his muscles trembling with leashed power held in check. She'd felt small and deliciously feminine in his arms, sensations she hadn't known in years.

Micah had reawakened a long-dormant part of her, a sensuality Bea had thought was lost forever. Now she realized it was still there and had simply been waiting for Micah's return.

Her response to his kiss had been instinctive. As soon as his lips had met hers, Bea's brain had signed off and her body had taken control. She'd lost herself in the moment, reveling in the reunion she'd never truly dared to hope for. Part of her wondered if she had imagined it, if the stress of the last few days had triggered a vivid dream so intense she thought it was real. But her lips ached slightly from Micah's attention, and there was a small mark on her chin where his stubble had grazed her skin. *Souvenirs*, she thought, her blood warming pleasantly at the realization that he'd left his mark on her, however subtle.

Last night had marked a shift in their relationship. They could no longer pretend to be polite strangers working together. Part of her was relieved that she didn't have to hide her feelings anymore. Now Micah knew she had missed him—*still* missed him—and unless she missed her guess, he felt the same way about her. The only question was, what were they going to do about it?

She hadn't known what to expect this morning, but Micah had acted completely normal, as if nothing unusual had happened last night. A small, cowardly part of her had felt relieved by his behavior. She was still processing Micah's kiss and her own conflicting emotions; she wasn't quite sure she was ready to talk at this point. Because, while her heart sang at the possibility of being with Micah again, her head was a bit more skeptical.

His breakup letter had been certain and final, shutting the door on their relationship. They hadn't spoken in years, so what had triggered his sudden change of heart? He'd never been the impulsive type, and she saw no signs that he had changed in that regard. Why, then, was he acting like he'd never sent that letter? And if he did regret breaking up with her, why hadn't he contacted her before now? She wasn't hard to find, and if Micah had wanted to get in touch with her, he would have been able to do so easily. The fact that he hadn't reached out made her wonder about his apparent feelings now. Was she making a mistake by opening her heart again? Would she be able to move on if Micah changed his mind once more?

"I just don't know," she muttered, gnawing on her thumbnail. There were so many things she needed to say, so many questions only Micah could answer. But could she trust him? Could she believe his responses? If he said he wanted her again, could she really risk her heart and soul on the one person who had hurt her so badly before?

She glanced down at Chunk, sleeping peacefully on the floor. He certainly trusted Micah—the strength of their bond was evident for everyone to see. Knowing he cared so much for the animal—and that the dog cared so much for him—made Bea feel a little bit better. Her mother had always insisted that dogs were excellent judges of character. Perhaps she should take Chunk's endorsement to heart and listen to what Micah had to say.

"It's just a conversation," she said softly. Talking to Micah didn't mean she was agreeing to go out on a date much less go to bed with him. Their chat would simply be a fact-finding mission, one that would hopefully clear up most of her questions. And if she didn't like his answers? She could walk away, no harm, no foul.

Bea nodded, satisfied with that plan. A talk would be a great way to clear the air, and it would do both of them a lot of good to lay their cards on the table. They'd spent the last ten years apart, with hurt feelings and a world of separate experiences shaping their lives. If they were ever going to overcome the obstacles of their past, they needed to be totally honest with each other.

The sooner the better.

Chapter 9

Micah leaned against the hood of his truck, watching the world go by as he made his calls.

"I think we should bring in Paulie Gains," he said, watching a group of children play on the swing set in the park just down the street from Bea's shop. A cluster of women sat on the benches nearby, chatting and sipping coffee, heads swiveling from conversation to kids and back again. It was shaping up to be a beautiful day, and Micah couldn't help but wish he had some time off so he could take Chunk for a nice hike.

Work first, he thought ruefully, tearing his gaze away from the laughing kids. *There will be plenty of nice days to enjoy once we catch the Groom Killer.*

"I agree." Brayden sighed, his frustration coming

through loud and clear over the line. "What time are you coming in today?"

"I should be there in a couple of hours," Micah said, glancing at the boutique. While he watched, two women, likely a mother and her daughter, walked into the shop. They were the first clients of the day, and he hoped, for Bea's sake, that they weren't coming in to cancel a dress order.

She'd tried to make light of the situation, but Micah could tell Bea's business was in trouble. The Groom Killer had everyone on edge, but engaged couples were especially concerned, and with good reason. There seemed to be no pattern to the victims at all, other than the fact the men were grooms or soon-to-be grooms. Since Bea's boutique was an integral part of the wedding scene in Red Ridge, she was an indirect victim of the killer's rampage.

All the more reason to wrap this case up quickly, he thought. He knew how important the shop was to her. It represented not only her grandmother but her independence from her father. If the business went under, the failure would affect her deeply.

"Carson and I will pick him up before you get here," Brayden said. "We'll wait for you to talk to him."

"I appreciate that," Micah replied. "I'll call you if anything comes up." He hung up and tucked the phone into his pocket, then pushed off the truck and headed to the café across the street.

Ten minutes later, he emerged with two travel mugs of coffee. He glanced at the park on his way back to the shop and did a double take. One of the Larson twins was standing in the park, deep in conversation with another man.

Intrigued, Micah set the drinks on the hood of his truck and leaned against the bumper, openly watching the two men. The Larson twins were well-known to the Red Ridge police department. They seemed to have their fingers in every unsavory pie, but the boys were slicker than an oil spill and the police had never been able to charge them with anything. Micah didn't expect to see anything incriminating, but it never hurt to pay attention...

The other man in the conversation turned, and Micah straightened as he recognized him. Thad Randall. The man was trouble—he'd been in and out of jail for petty theft and more recently for drug dealing. Why was a Larson brother talking to this guy?

And just which Larson was he looking at? He studied the man a moment, looking for clues. Evan Larson, he decided. Both of the brothers were snappy dressers, but while Noel Larson wore his expensive suits like a second skin, Evan always looked a bit uncomfortable, as if he was wearing his father's clothes. Micah got the impression Evan would be more comfortable in jeans and a T-shirt, but the Teflon Twins had an image to maintain and that meant both of them had to dress the part.

Evan caught Micah staring and frowned. He said something to Thad, and the two men glared at Micah. Thad looked like he was going to walk over, so Micah made a show of taking his badge off his belt and polishing it on his shirt.

Thad seemed to shrink a little, and Evan's expression morphed from one of brash confidence to open hostility. Micah gave the pair a cheery wave, and snapped a few photos with his phone's camera. It wasn't a crime for Evan to talk to Thad, but Micah doubted the two were old friends catching up in the park on a sunny day. Something was going on between the two men, and Micah suspected whatever they were doing was on the wrong side of the law.

He wished he could get close enough to eavesdrop on the conversation, but now that both men had spotted him that was out of the question. In any event, it didn't matter—they weren't sticking around. Thad was already walking away, and Evan shot Micah a hateful glare as he turned and walked in the opposite direction. Pretty suspicious behavior for what he was sure Evan Larson would claim was an innocent conversation, but Micah didn't have the grounds to detain him and ask about it.

Frustration built in his chest as he slipped his phone into his pocket and picked up the travel mugs. He knew Evan Larson—and by extension, his brother—were up to something, but he couldn't prove it. And the most galling part of it all was that the men had the audacity to conduct their dealings out in public, right under his nose. It seemed like the twins went out of their way to deliberately taunt the police, and he got the feeling the brothers saw it all as a game.

"One thing at a time," he muttered as he walked

to the door of Bea's boutique. First, solve the Groom Killer case. Then he could turn his attention to the Teflon Twins and hopefully dig up something on them that would finally stick.

"Should I just wait in the break room again?"

Micah shook his head as he led Bea and Chunk through the clusters of desks in the main squad room. "No, I'd actually like you to listen to what this guy has to say. It might trigger a memory that will help the investigation."

"Okay." She sounded doubtful and a little worried, clearly uncomfortable with the idea.

"No one will see you," he assured her. "The room has a two-way mirror, so you can watch from next door."

"Like on TV?" she asked, brightening a bit.

Micah nodded, smiling at her reaction. "Yes, just like that." He made a quick stop at his desk and pointed at Chunk's bed. "Rest," he commanded. Chunk obediently climbed onto the pad and turned his customary circles before settling down with a sigh.

"He's such a good dog," Bea said, her tone affectionate.

Micah felt a surge of warmth at her words. The fact that Bea clearly liked his partner made him happy, and he felt himself softening even further toward her. He still wasn't sure if he could trust her, but anyone who liked Chunk was a good judge of character. And the dog clearly adored her, which was another point in her favor...

His emotions must have shown on his face, because Bea looked up at him with a hopeful expression. "Do you think we could talk later?" She sounded a little shy, as if she was worried about his reaction to the simple question.

Nervous energy sprang to life in Micah's stomach. He knew they needed to talk about what had happened last night, and where they wanted to go from here. But he'd hoped to have a little more time to get his thoughts in order before starting that conversation.

And maybe he would. Bea wasn't asking him to drop everything and talk now. She'd said *later*, which implied at least several hours, if not a few days. Plenty of time for him to figure things out.

He hoped.

Micah nodded as he guided her down the hall to the interrogation rooms. "Yes. That sounds like a good idea."

Bea emitted a small sigh, her shoulders relaxing. "Okay," she said softly. "Later, then."

Micah ushered her into the small viewing room. "Here we are," he said. "I'll be just next door, talking to the witness. Remember, we can't see or hear you, so if you need to get my attention for any reason, tap on the glass."

"All right."

"I'm going to ask him a lot of questions about what he saw. He's a witness to the first killing. Pay close attention, because it's possible he might say something that helps you remember more details from the night of your attack."

"I'll do my best." She glanced into the other room, a determined expression on her face.

Affection rose in his chest, making him want to hug her. She genuinely wanted to help him, which was more than he could say for many of the people connected to this case. He glanced at Paulie and heaved a mental sigh. The man hadn't been terribly cooperative the first time they'd questioned him; given his defensive posture and sour expression, Micah didn't think he'd be too forthcoming now.

Still, he had to try.

He left Bea in the observation room and stepped into the hall to find Carson and Brayden already waiting for him. "Did he give you any trouble when you picked him up?"

Brayden shook his head. "Nah. Mouthed off a little, but he had to put on a show for his friends."

"All right, then. You guys ready?"

"Let's get to it," Carson responded.

Micah opened the door to the interrogation room, making Paulie jump. He covered it with a sneer as he watched the three detectives file in. "Three against one? That hardly seems fair."

"Works for me," Micah said, trying to keep his tone friendly.

Gains shifted in his seat, his eyes darting from Micah to Carson to Brayden and back again. The man was clearly uncomfortable, which in his case meant he probably had something to hide. Paulie wasn't one of Red Ridge's more upstanding citizens; he'd had several brushes with the law over the years. Mostly little stuff like petty theft or public intoxication—never anything that rose to the level of a felony. But Micah had always suspected Paulie's lack of a serious record was due more to luck than the man's own behavior.

"So, why am I here?" he asked, breaking the silence. "What's so important you had to haul me down to the station, instead of just having a friendly chat at the bar?"

Micah and Brayden took the two chairs across from Paulie, while Carson stood in the corner. "We'd like you to recount what you saw the night Bo Gage was murdered."

Paulie's face scrunched up. "Recount?"

"Tell us about it," Brayden clarified. "We want to hear your story again."

"Oh, is that all?" Gains said, the tension leaving his body as he relaxed into his chair. "Why didn't you just say so in the first place?"

Micah and Brayden exchanged a look. "What did you think we wanted to talk to you about?" Micah asked innocently.

Paulie flapped his hand, waving off the question. "Nothing. My imagination just gets to working overtime, you know." His laugh was forced and nervous, and it didn't fool anyone. Micah made a mental note to keep tabs on Gains once they were done here. If he tried to probe into the man's business now, he wouldn't get any answers regarding the Groom Killer case. Since that was his priority, he'd just have to ignore whatever it was Paulie was up to for the time being.

"Tell us what you saw that night," Carson said, his voice quiet and commanding. Bo Gage, the first victim, was Carson's half brother. Micah knew it had to be difficult for him to work on this case, but Carson had never once complained about the long hours or the investigative dead ends.

Gains nodded. "Yeah, sure. Well, it's like I said at the time. I saw a woman running away from the bar around six thirty, six forty-five. Long, curly red hair. Dead ringer for Demi Colton, if you'll pardon the expression." He glanced quickly at Carson, then away again.

"Did you hear her speak?" Brayden asked.

Paulie shook his head. "Nah. I wasn't close enough for that."

"But you were close enough to see that she had red hair, even though it was getting dark?" Micah said.

Gains shifted in his seat. "Uh…well, uh, yeah. She…" He trailed off, and Micah could practically see the wheels turning in Paulie's head as he struggled to come up with a plausible explanation. "She ran under a street light and that's when I noticed her hair color," he finished triumphantly. "So that's how I know."

"I see," Micah commented. "I don't suppose you noticed anything else?"

Paulie looked at him blankly. "Like what?"

Micah shrugged. "Oh, I don't know. Maybe she was wearing perfume?"

"Could be," Paulie said. "I'll have to think about it."

Brayden leaned forward. "You know, Paulie, I have to say your testimony is a little unusual."

Gains eyed him suspiciously, his guard snapping into place. "Oh? Why's that?"

"Well, usually when a witness talks to us, their story changes slightly every time they repeat it. Not the main details, but the words they use. They might say 'the guy was wearing a blue hat' the first time, and by the tenth time they're calling it a baseball cap."

"So?" Paulie's tone was defensive, and Micah noted a flicker of fear in his eyes. "What's that got to do with me?"

"Every time we've talked to you, you've used the exact same words in the exact same order," Brayden said. "Almost like you've memorized your statement. I'm just wondering why you would do that."

"I didn't."

"Paulie," Micah said, careful to keep his voice soothing. "If there's something you want to tell us, now would be a good time."

Gains shifted his gaze to Micah. He was looking more and more like a cornered mouse trying to escape a pride of lions. Beads of sweat glistened on his forehead, and he swiped a hand across his chin. "Like what?"

"Did someone tell you what to say?"

Paulie didn't respond right away, so Micah pressed a little. "Look, I know times are tough. Maybe someone offered you money to say you saw something that night? It happens. All you had to do was tell us about the redhead by the bar. No big deal, right?"

Gains nodded slowly, looking almost hypnotized. Micah's heart jumped—he was getting close to the truth, he could *feel* it. "Is that what happened, Paulie? Did someone tell you what to say?"

Brayden shifted in his chair, causing it to drag across the floor. The sound wasn't very loud, but it was enough to get Paulie's attention. He snapped free of his trance and shook his head vigorously. "No. I saw what I saw. No one paid me anything."

Micah leaned back with a mental sigh. It was obvious Paulie was lying, but unless Gains flipped on whoever had paid him to give a false statement, Micah had no way to prove it.

Paulie crossed his arms, his expression obstinate as he looked from Micah to Brayden. "Can I go now?"

Micah fought the urge to lean across the table and shake the man. "Paulie—" he began, hoping to reconnect. He'd been so close to the truth before. If he could just get Paulie to listen to him again…

Gains shook his head. "I told you everything I know. I don't have anything new to say."

No one replied right away, which seemed to fuel Paulie's determination. "I don't care how long you keep me here. My story isn't going to change."

No kidding, Micah thought sourly. That much was clear.

It was time to lay it all out for the man. "Look, here's the deal. If you're lying, you need to tell us. It's not too late for you to come forward, and we can help you make things right. But if you don't…" Micah trailed off and shook his head. "If you let this go on much longer, you're tying my hands. I want to help you, I really do. But you have to help me, too."

Gains sat stone-faced. "I got nothing to say. Can I go now?"

"Yeah," Micah said with a sigh. "We're done here." He pushed to his feet, sending his chair to the floor with a crash.

Gains flinched as he stood. Micah took one of his cards from his pocket and held it out. Paulie looked at his hand suspiciously. "What's that?"

Micah summoned his dwindling patience. "My card. In case you remember anything. Or decide you want to talk to me again." It was a long shot, but maybe once Gains had had a little time to think, he'd reconsider his lies.

Paulie shook his head. "Nah. I don't need that. I told you before. I don't know anything else."

Micah stepped forward, triggering a small squeak of alarm from Paulie. He tucked the card into the man's shirt pocket and gave his chest a little tap. "Humor me," Micah said quietly. He bared his teeth in a fierce grin and felt a spurt of satisfaction as Gains swallowed with an audible gulp.

"C'mon," Carson said from the corner. "I'll escort you out."

Gaines nodded and moved to follow Carson. But he kept his eyes on Micah the whole time, as if to assure himself that Micah wasn't going to follow him.

Maybe that's the way to get through to him, Micah

mused. *If he fears me more than the person who paid him, I might be able to get a name out of him.*

As a general rule, Micah didn't like to use fear as a weapon. But in this case, he was willing to make an exception...

"I'm so sorry."

He turned to find Brayden staring at the table, his shoulders slumped.

"Don't worry about it," Micah said kindly. He was disappointed in the outcome of the interview, but taking his frustration out on Brayden wasn't going to help.

Brayden glanced up. "I shouldn't have moved. You had him. He was about to talk." He shook his head, and for a second, Micah was afraid his friend was going to be sick.

"It's okay," Micah said, faking a confidence he didn't feel. "We'll get him again. He just needs some time to think things over."

"You think?" There was a note of hope in Brayden's voice that Micah couldn't bear to squash.

"Yeah," he said. "In the meantime, why don't you make Gains your pet project? Really dig into his past and his contacts. See if you can come up with a list of possible suspects who would have a reason to pay him to lie about what he saw."

"Done," Brayden said. He straightened, a glint of determination in his eyes. "I'll make this right."

Micah smiled. "I know you will." He could have investigated Paulie himself, but he knew asking Brayden to do it was the better choice. Micah didn't hold it against him, but he knew his friend felt bad about his mistake during the interview. Digging into Paulie's business was his opportunity to earn a little redemption and hopefully restore his confidence.

Micah was no stranger to guilt and self-recrimination. He'd spent months after the ambush nearly paralyzed with indecision, second-guessing his every choice, no matter how small or insignificant. And while Brayden's mistake hadn't cost any lives, Micah knew that once the seed of doubt had sprouted, it grew quickly.

A soft knock on the doorframe pulled him out of his head. Bea stood in the hall, looking hesitant.

"Can I come in? I figured since he was gone it was okay for me to move, but if this is a bad time…" She trailed off, glancing from Micah to Brayden.

"No, it's fine." Micah gestured for her to join them. "I didn't mean to leave you alone that long. Sorry."

She shrugged. "It's fine. I know you're busy."

"Well, that was a colossal waste of time," Carson said sourly as he walked in. "I thought you had him there for a minute, but then—" He broke off, as if suddenly realizing Brayden was still in the room.

A flush of color climbed up Brayden's neck, but he didn't respond.

"We gave him something to think about," Micah said, trying to salvage the conversation. He turned to Bea. "I don't suppose you remembered anything new?"

She shook her head, her expression apologetic. "No. I'm sorry."

"Don't be. It's pretty clear Gains is lying, so I wouldn't expect his statement to shed any light on your attack."

"What happens now?" she asked.

Micah sighed and ran a hand through his hair. "Now I start looking at our victim, Joey McBurn. Hopefully we can figure out how he wound up in the crosshairs of the killer."

"Let me know if you need help," Carson said. "I'm still chasing down leads from Bo's murder, but since these cases seem to be connected I'm happy to share what I know if you think it will help."

"Thanks," Micah said, appreciating the offer. The squad had a weekly meeting where everyone briefed the team about each case, but it wouldn't hurt to pick Carson's brain.

"Let's get back to it," he said, glancing around the room. Carson and Brayden nodded, and they all filed back into the hall, headed to the main bullpen and their respective desks.

Three grooms had been killed in as many months. And now the killer was targeting witnesses. That kind of escalation wasn't a good sign, and the pressure for answers was mounting.

Tick-tock, tick-tock. Could he solve this case before someone else died? Or had the Groom Killer already selected the next victim?

Chapter 10

It was late afternoon when Micah finally pushed back from his desk. "I can't stare at this screen any longer," he announced, rubbing his eyes with the heels of his hands. "I need to get outside."

"That sounds good to me," Bea replied. While Micah had been working, she'd been going over the accounts for the boutique. There was far too much red on the screen for her liking, and while she knew closing her laptop wasn't going to make her business problems go away, a distraction would be nice right about now.

"I need to take Chunk for a long walk," he said. "I can leave you here at the station and pick you up later, if you like."

"Actually, can I go with you?" In all the chaos

of the past few days, she hadn't been to the gym. It would feel good to stretch her legs and breathe fresh air. And maybe she and Micah could talk about what had happened between them last night...

Micah shrugged. "Works for me." He stood and Chunk lifted his head from the bed, his expression hopeful. "Let's go, buddy."

Half an hour later, Micah and Bea had both changed into T-shirts and sneakers. The three of them stepped off the porch, Chunk tugging eagerly at the leash as they walked. The dog wagged his tail happily, sniffing industriously at everything they passed.

"He seems to be enjoying himself," Bea said.

Micah smiled indulgently as he looked at the dog. "Yeah. I usually walk him every day, but our schedule has been a little off lately."

There was no censure in his voice, but Bea felt her face flush nonetheless. "Sorry about that."

"It's not your fault," he said easily. "You have nothing to apologize for."

They walked in silence for a few moments. The sun was warm on Bea's shoulders, and she felt the tension draining from her muscles as she moved. Their pace was steady but not strenuous—they couldn't walk too quickly, since Chunk had a tendency to stop every few feet for a more thorough investigation of some interesting bush or clump of flowers. Micah tolerated these delays with patience, letting the dog sniff his fill before urging him to move on.

She studied Micah, trying to determine if it was a good time to bring up last night's kiss. He seemed relaxed, much happier than he'd been before they'd left the station. Now was probably as good a time as any to start the conversation; if she put it off much longer, she might lose her nerve.

Butterflies filled her stomach as she gathered her courage. She took a deep breath, searching for the right words to say—she wanted to open this discussion on a good note so she didn't make him immediately uncomfortable. If Micah shut down, she'd never get any answers.

"So…" She trailed off, feeling foolish. Then she shook her head. *Just go for it.* "What happened last night?"

If Micah was surprised by her question, he didn't show it. "I kissed you."

Oh, is that all? His tone was casual, as if he did that sort of thing all the time. A kernel of doubt manifested in her mind. Maybe the kiss hadn't affected him as much as it had her…

"Yeah, I noticed that." She tried to keep her voice light. If Micah didn't think the kiss had meant anything, she wasn't going to clue him in on her feelings. She wasn't in the mood to get her heart broken again, thank you very much.

Micah cleared his throat. "I'm sorry about that. I let my emotions take control, and I shouldn't have."

Her heart lifted at his words. If he had emotions where she was concerned, perhaps he wasn't so unaffected after all. "I'm not upset."

A muscle in his jaw tightened. "I am," he muttered.

Bea's frustration mounted. This wasn't going well

at all. She hadn't meant to make Micah feel bad—she'd simply wanted to talk now that they were both calm. She took a deep breath and tried again. "I meant what I said last night. I miss you."

He was silent a moment, the only sounds the crunch of their footsteps on the grassy trail and the chuffs from Chunk as he explored the terrain. When it became clear he wasn't going to answer her right away, her exasperation overcame her patience. "Do you feel the same way about me?"

"Does it matter?" he said.

"Yes. It matters to me."

"All right. Then, yes, I do miss you." He huffed out a sigh. "Are you happy now?"

Part of her did rejoice to hear her feelings were reciprocated. But she didn't understand why Micah seemed so bothered by his admission. She had confessed her feelings first, laying the groundwork for him to do the same. He didn't have to fear her rejection, so why was he so upset?

"It doesn't sound like you're happy," she said. "What's going on?"

Chunk stopped to explore a rather large bush and Micah turned to face her. His green eyes flashed with emotion—anger? Sadness? She couldn't be sure.

"What is it you want from me, Bea?" he asked. "Isn't it enough to know I never stopped thinking about you? Do you want me on my knees—will that satisfy you?"

His outburst stunned her. Where was this reaction coming from? She hadn't asked him to break up with her, and she certainly wasn't asking him to grovel for her forgiveness. Although the idea was a bit tempting, in light of his current response…

"I don't know what you're talking about," she said, her temper sharpening her tone. "I just thought we should discuss what happened between us last night. Clearly, you don't feel the same way. Forget I ever brought it up."

She turned and began walking again, striding away from his shocked expression. She didn't make it far before she heard the shuffle of his footsteps. He caught up to her quickly, her angry pace no match for his long-legged stride. He fell into step beside her but didn't speak for a moment.

"I'm sorry," he said quietly. "I don't know what to say, or how to process all this."

"I don't either," she admitted. "I didn't ask to feel this way."

His smile was tinged with sadness. "I can imagine. You probably never thought you'd see me again after you sent that letter."

Bea frowned as his words sank in. None of the letters she'd written to him during his basic training had contained anything angry or hurtful. What was he talking about?

"What letter?"

He shot her a knowing look. "Oh, come on. You can't be serious."

She stopped walking, and after a few steps he stopped, too. "What letter, Micah?"

He lifted one eyebrow and pressed his lips together. "Your Dear John letter. The only one you ever sent me while I was away. Was it really so insignificant to you that you don't remember?"

Bea felt as though all the blood in her body was racing south, pooling on the ground beneath her. A sense of numbness claimed her feet, then her legs, spreading up and through her body with every beat of her heart. Her knees gave out, and she dropped to the ground.

Micah was at her side in an instant, kneeling next to her. "Hey," he said, placing his hand on her shoulder. "What's happening? Talk to me."

Chunk nosed at her neck and the cold pressure helped break through her distress. "I never sent you a Dear John letter," she said, her voice shaking.

Micah rocked back on his heels, frowning. "Yeah, you did. You said you didn't want to be a soldier's wife and that I shouldn't try to contact you."

"No." She shook her head so hard the ends of her hair slapped against her cheeks with small, sharp stings. "I never wrote that."

"Okay." He nodded, but she heard the doubt in his voice.

She reached out and grabbed his shirt with both hands, gripping tightly. "I wrote to you every day," she said, enunciating every word. "But I never sent you a breakup letter. That's what you did to me."

"What?" His expression morphed from concerned to confused. "What are you talking about?"

"You sent *me* a letter," she said firmly. "You told

me you didn't want a wife holding you back and that I should find someone else."

Micah blinked, clearly taken aback. "That's crazy," he said slowly. "I didn't have any time to write to you, and I certainly wouldn't have broken up with you in a letter. I would have called or waited until I came back from basic training so we could talk in person."

Tears stung her eyes as she pictured his handwriting sloping across the page. "I tried to call you after I read what you'd written, but I couldn't get through. Since I wasn't family, they wouldn't let me talk to you."

He shook his head. "I don't understand." He pushed to his feet and began to pace, clearly agitated. "This doesn't make any sense. I got a letter from you—it was in your handwriting, with your return address, postmarked from Red Ridge. And you're telling me you received a letter I never wrote."

She nodded. "Do you still have it?"

"Yeah." He stopped walking and cleared his throat. "I do, actually. Don't know why I kept the damn thing, but I figured it was the last time I'd ever hear from you. Made me a little sentimental, I guess."

Bea exhaled in relief. "I still have my letter, too. It's in my desk drawer at home."

"You up for a little field trip?"

She nodded, her heart lifting. "Yes. I need to know what's going on."

"Let's go," he said, his eyes shining with determination. "This is one mystery we can solve tonight."

* * *

Micah stared at the piece of paper in his hand, reading the words over and over again.

His heart twisted at the callous, impersonal message. It was all too easy to imagine Bea reading this alone, her heart breaking as she tried to understand why the man she loved was ending things between them. For a split second, he was disappointed she had thought him capable of breaking up with her via a letter, but then he reminded himself he'd thought the same of her when he'd gotten his own message.

"This… I never wrote this."

Bea glanced up from the letter he'd given her to read, her eyes wide. "I didn't write this, either." She shook her head and returned her gaze to the paper. "It looks a lot like my handwriting, but it's just a little bit off. The *T*s aren't quite right, and the curve of the *S* is wrong, as well."

Micah glanced back at the letter in his hand. "Mine looks like that as well," he said, realization dawning. "The writing is close, but it's not exact." He read through the message once again, trying to see it through Bea's eyes. It certainly looked legitimate. And in the heat of the moment, with her emotions high, it made sense she hadn't stopped to compare the letter to some of the other cards he'd sent her during their relationship. He certainly hadn't thought to do that at the time. "I can see why you believed I wrote this," he said softly.

She nodded, her hazel eyes full of sadness. "Likewise." She pursed her lips, exhaling in a long sigh.

"My God," she said, shaking her head. "How much time did we lose? When I think about what our lives would be like now if this had never happened…" She trailed off and swiped at her eyes.

Micah nodded, not trusting himself to speak. Bea was right. They'd probably be married by now, maybe with a child or two. He certainly wouldn't have spent the past ten years trying to put his heart back together, wondering if he'd ever be able to find another woman who fit him so perfectly.

He reached out, needing to touch her. She moved readily into his arms, snuggling up against his chest as her breath hitched. "Hey." He stroked her hair, running his hand down her back in a soothing caress. A sense of calm filled him as he held her. Last night's kiss had been part reunion, part punishment. But this embrace was different. All his anger toward Bea, the years of hurt feelings and painful memories—it all melted away, like storm clouds disappearing on a sunny day. His feelings for her, including the love he'd thought he'd buried for good, rose to the surface, rushing to fill the empty spaces in his soul.

It was more than he'd ever dared hope for. In his wildest imaginings, Micah had never dreamed this moment was possible. He inhaled deeply, drawing her familiar floral scent deep into his lungs, needing to convince himself this was truly happening. Bea was here. She was real. And she had never stopped loving him.

"I'm so sorry," he whispered into her hair. Guilt

nipped at the edges of his happiness, reminding him they still had a lot to talk about.

Bea pulled back and looked up at him, her eyes bright with tears. "Why are you sorry? You didn't send the letter. This isn't your fault."

Micah took a deep breath, enjoying the feel of her curves as his chest expanded. "I know. But I thought the worst of you. I should have made an effort to contact you, to ask for an explanation. But I let my hurt pride keep me from reaching out, and I was repeating that same mistake now."

"What do you mean?"

He shook his head, feeling his cheeks heat with shame. "You told me last night that you missed me. I didn't want to admit I felt the same way. I held on to my anger and hurt feelings, thinking you didn't deserve an explanation. If you hadn't forced me to talk, well…" He trailed off, his stomach twisting at the thought of how close he'd come to missing the opportunity to set things right between them.

Bea reached up and cupped his cheek with her hand. Her palm was warm and soft against his skin, and he leaned into her touch. "Don't beat yourself up about it," she said softly. "You had every right to respond the way you did."

"You went through the same thing, but you handled it a lot better," he pointed out. "It took a lot of courage to say what you did last night, and to talk about it again today. I don't think I could have been that brave."

She laughed, the sadness leaving her eyes. "That's

funny. You're a former Army Ranger and a police officer, and you think you're not brave?" She shook her head and gave his arm a squeeze. "Don't sell yourself short."

Micah tightened his embrace, needing her to understand. "That's different. It's one thing to put yourself in physical danger. It's quite another to risk your heart."

Bea grew quiet, digesting his words. "That's true," she said finally. "We both took a risk today. And I think it paid off."

A small flame kindled to life in his chest, spreading tendrils of warmth through his body. The sensation was unfamiliar, and it took him a moment to realize what he was feeling.

Happiness.

True, unadulterated happiness. The kind of joy that only comes along every once in a while.

His life hadn't been all doom and gloom since their breakup; he'd had moments of elation over the past ten years. Getting accepted to Ranger school and, later, making it through the K-9 training program. Goofing around with Duke and then Chunk. And a few moments of levity with his fellow Rangers and his coworkers on the force. But this was different. Before, his enjoyment of life had always felt incomplete, like he couldn't celebrate with his whole being because he was missing parts of himself. But now, for the first time in a long time, Micah felt whole again.

"Does this mean you're willing to give me another chance?" He held his breath even as he asked the question. But recent events had driven home the importance of risking his heart. He felt like a dog exposing his belly, but he needed Bea to know he trusted her and wanted her in his life.

"Only if you'll do the same for me," she said softly.

Micah's heart leaped at her words. Before he could think better of it, he dropped his head and claimed her mouth with his own.

This time, he wasn't afraid to show her how much he wanted her. He lowered his guard, worshiping her with his lips and tongue. Micah wanted Bea to feel cherished and appreciated, to know his fire for her hadn't dimmed despite their years apart.

After a moment, he pulled back to draw a breath. Bea slowly opened her eyes, her gaze dreamy as she stared up at him. Micah wanted nothing more than to sweep her into his arms and carry her to the bedroom down the hall, but he forced his muscles to relax.

"Sorry," he said, his voice husky. "I think you know how much I want you, but I just realized it's been ten years. We should probably pace ourselves, don't you think?"

Disappointment flashed in her hazel eyes, but she nodded. "I suppose so." Her kiss-swollen lips curved up in a sly grin. "But feel free to kiss me like that anytime you want."

His groin throbbed with every beat of his heart, and he almost gave in to temptation. Fortunately, his brain caught up with him. *No*, he thought, with more than a little regret. *We need to do this the right way.* Micah wanted to build a new relationship with Bea, one that would last the rest of his life. That meant taking the time to get to know her again, to discover the woman she'd become. As much as he would enjoy getting physically reacquainted with her, it was more important they repair their emotional connection first.

"You've got a deal," he said.

"Excellent." She stepped back, glancing at the letter on the desk. Her smile faded as she stared at the paper.

Micah touched her cheek. "Forget about it," he said softly. "We know the truth. Don't let past mistakes bring you down now."

Bea shook her head. "I won't. But I just wish I could go back in time and change things."

"I know the feeling," he said, thinking of all the times he'd wished to do the same in the aftermath of the ambush. How many lives would have been saved, how many men would have emerged unscathed if only he had made a different choice? He'd nearly driven himself mad with the what-ifs and alternative possibilities. It was a struggle he wouldn't wish on his worst enemy, and he definitely didn't want Bea to fall down that particular rabbit hole of self-doubt and recrimination.

"Please believe me when I tell you thinking that way will only hurt you in the long run."

She studied his face, and for a second, Micah felt like she could see through him. "Are you talking about the ambush?"

Shock hit him before he remembered he'd told her about Duke's injuries. At some point, he would probably need to tell her more details about the attack, but he wasn't feeling up for it right now. So he simply nodded.

"Do you still blame yourself?" Her voice was calm and soothing, and the stillness of her apartment made the moment seem almost confessional. In that instant, Micah knew he could tell Bea anything and she wouldn't flinch or shy away from him.

It was on the tip of his tongue to explain exactly what had happened, but as he looked at her upturned face, he realized he didn't want to fill her head with images of war and death, of men lying broken and bloody in the desert sand. Living through it had been bad enough; he didn't want her touched by those moments, however removed they now were from that time and place.

"Sometimes," he said, clearing his throat in an effort to dislodge the lump that always appeared when he thought of that day. "There was an after-action report, and my superiors said it wasn't my fault. But it's hard not to wonder if I made the wrong choices in the heat of the moment."

Bea tilted her head to the side. "I'm not going to pretend to understand the nuances of the army," she said. "But an after-action report sounds pretty serious to me. It doesn't seem like the kind of thing your bosses would sugarcoat in an effort to spare your feelings."

Micah laughed at the ridiculous thought. "It's not."

She shrugged. "Then it sounds like you can trust

that no one was lying or brushing aside your mistakes to make you feel better."

"No, they definitely were not."

She shrugged again, in a kind of there-you-go gesture. He smiled.

"What?" she asked, sounding a little wary.

"Nothing. It's just—do you know how many therapy sessions it took for me to reach that understanding? And you figured it out in less than five minutes."

Bea's eyes widened. "Oh, Micah, I didn't mean to sound so flippant. It wasn't my intention to discount your experiences—"

He waved away her protest. "I'm not upset with you. I just think it's funny how you were able to cut right to the heart of my issues, without even knowing the nitty-gritty details."

"I get the impression you don't want to talk about the details. But if you do, I'll be here. I want to know everything that happened to you while we were apart."

"I'm glad you feel that way, because I want the same." He reached out and took the letter from her. "So let's tear these up and start fresh."

"Yes to the starting fresh, but no to the tearing up." She took the letter back and gathered up his, as well. "I'm not willing to let this go quite so easily."

He had a sneaking suspicion Bea's father had orchestrated the whole mix-up, but he didn't want to suggest it. Fenwick Colton was a Grade-A asshole, but he was still Bea's father, and Micah didn't want to come between them. "Are you sure you don't want to just put this behind us and move forward?"

Bea shook her head, a stubborn glint in her eyes. "No. I'm afraid I'm not that mature. I want answers, and I know exactly where to go to find them."

Chapter 11

The next morning dawned clear and bright, the exact opposite of Bea's mood. Micah pulled up in front of the multistory headquarters of Colton Energy and turned to face her.

"Are you sure about this? I'm happy to come with you."

Bea shook her head. "I need to do this by myself."

"Okay." Micah's green eyes were kind as he watched her. "If that's what you think is best." He reached over and took her hand, giving it a reassuring squeeze. "I'll be thinking about you the whole time."

She smiled, feeling his concern like an embrace. "I know." She reached for the door handle, then paused. "Can I ask you one thing before I go in?"

"Anything."

"How are you so calm right now? I am spitting mad, but you seem almost blasé about the situation."

Micah chuckled. "Oh, believe me, I'm furious. But I care more about you than I do about getting revenge." He pulled her hand to his mouth for a kiss. "Promise me you won't do anything you'll regret. I know he hurt you, but he's still your father."

Bea lifted one eyebrow. "I don't know if I can make that promise," she said, "but I will try. How's that?"

Micah nodded. "I'll settle for it."

She leaned over and pressed her mouth to his, wanting to carry the feel of his lips against hers when she walked in to confront her father. Then she reached back to scratch Chunk behind the ears and opened the door. "I'll call you."

Micah waved and waited at the curb until she had walked through the front doors of the building. Bea paused in the lobby, watching him drive away. Part of her wanted him with her now, but she knew she would have better luck talking to her father alone. He'd never liked Micah, but until this moment, Bea hadn't realized just how deep her father's hatred ran.

Micah hadn't been happy about the idea of leaving her alone, but she'd insisted. So Micah had made some calls, arranging for one of the building security officers to escort her everywhere. Bea considered it overkill, but Micah hadn't been willing to budge on the issue.

She rode the elevator up to the top floor with her escort, taking the opportunity to study her reflection in the closed doors. She'd opted for a casual look today, just jeans and a sweater. She smiled to herself, knowing her father would take offense to her wardrobe. Fenwick thought proper ladies wore skirts, which was why Colton Energy had a strict dress code for its employees. Women were free to wear whatever professional clothing they liked, but the smart ones quickly figured out their fortunes improved when they donned skirts in favor of pants.

Just one more way he tries to control people, Bea thought to herself.

The elevator stopped and she stepped into the lobby of the executive floor. A large mahogany desk sat at the far side of the room, and behind the desk was the entrance to her father's office.

Bea walked forward, her feet sinking into the thick nap of the carpet. A middle-aged blonde woman sat behind the secretary's desk and smiled as Bea approached.

"Miss Colton, what a pleasure. Your father is currently in a meeting, but if you'd like to have a seat—" the secretary gestured to a row of padded chairs lined up along the wall "—I'll let him know you're here."

Bea smiled and nodded, not surprised the woman had recognized her even though they'd never met before. Her father had a large family portrait hanging in his office to lend credence to his claim of being a family man. It stood to reason his secretary had learned the names of Bea and her siblings, knowing she might one day be called upon to use them.

Bea sat in one of the chairs and crossed her legs,

pretending to relax. The secretary stood and walked over. "May I offer you something to drink?" she asked politely.

"Coffee would be lovely," Bea replied. The woman nodded and set off down the hall, presumably toward a break room. Bea waited until she was gone, then stood and walked into her father's office.

He was in a meeting, that much was true. Fenwick sat at the head of a conference table, listening to a man in a suit drone on about capital investment strategies. Bea closed his office door with a thud, and every head in the room swiveled toward her at the interruption.

If Fenwick was surprised to see her, he didn't show it. His eyes flicked over her appearance, and even from this distance she could see the corners of his mouth turn down in disapproval. She met his gaze and raised one eyebrow in challenge. Her father turned back to the table and took command of the meeting once more.

"Gentlemen, I appreciate your counsel. I apologize for the interruption, but let's pick this back up again later."

There were murmurs of agreement, coupled with the sound of shuffling papers as everyone gathered their supplies and stood. One by one, the men in suits filed out of the office. Several of them cast curious glances in Bea's direction as they walked past, but she ignored them.

The secretary burst into the room, her expression

panicked. "Mr. Colton, I do apologize," she said, sounding breathless. "I asked her to wait—"

Fenwick waved her off. "It's fine," he said, forcing a smile. "I always have time for my daughter."

He waited until everyone had left, then walked over to his desk and sat in the padded leather throne. "That was quite an entrance you made," he said, dropping all pretense of affection. "What the hell gives you the right to barge into my office and disrupt one of my meetings?"

Bea stalked forward, rounding his desk until she stood next to him. Her father's eyes widened slightly at the intrusion into his personal space. He had thought she would stay on the other side of his desk like a good little girl, giving him the advantage. Little did he know she was done being predictable.

She pulled the letters out of her purse and flung them in his lap. "What the hell gives you the right to interfere in my life?"

Fenwick picked up the pages and scanned them. "I don't know what you're talking about," he said in a bored tone.

"Yes, you do. You orchestrated this whole thing. Tell me, how long did it take you to find someone to forge my handwriting and Micah's?"

Her father narrowed his eyes, clearly calculating his next move. He carefully folded the pages and handed them back to her. "Not long," he finally said. "It pays to have connections."

His confession made her sick to her stomach. When she had seen Micah's letter and realized it was

a forgery, she'd immediately thought her father was
responsible. Still, a small part of her had held out hope
that he wasn't behind this deception. She'd wanted
to believe her dad wasn't capable of hurting her like
that, but his casual admission was like a knife to her
heart, cutting through any remaining affection she
had for the man.

She schooled her features, determined not to let
him see her pain. "Why did you do it?"

Fenwick rolled his eyes. "Why do you think? He's
not right for you. He never was."

"That wasn't your decision to make," she said
levelly. Her throat ached to scream at him, and she
was proud of herself for keeping her temper under
control. If she showed any kind of emotion, her
father would consider it a victory.

"Of course it was!" He shoved to his feet, forcing
Bea to take a step back. "Micah Shaw is nothing but
a low-class boy who could never give you the kind of
life you need. I saved you from making a huge mistake. Just look at his father—the man drank away his
paychecks in the Pour House every other Friday night.
The apple doesn't fall far from the tree, trust me."

Bea shook her head, amazed at the venom in
her father's voice. "How dare you," she said softly.
"Micah put on a uniform and served his country with
honor. Now he's back, protecting the people of this
city from danger. He's a better man than you could
ever hope to be."

"Oh, please. He signed up for the army because he
didn't have any other prospects. And he came back

here because he inherited his aunt's house. Do you honestly think he could afford his own home otherwise?"

She took a step back, needing to distance herself from this man. She'd thought she'd known her father, but now she realized he was a complete stranger. "It all comes down to money with you, doesn't it?"

"How do you think this world works, little girl?" Fenwick snapped. "You've never wanted for anything a day in your life. Did you think your needs were magically met? No! I provided you with everything, and I did it with money. I would have thought you'd have figured that out by now, since you're playing at being a businesswoman. But you never did have a head for numbers."

Rage filled her chest, making it hard to breathe. She stood frozen in place, her anger locking her muscles into rigidity so that she couldn't move. For the first time in her life, Bea felt the urge to strike someone.

"Why are you bringing this up now, years later?" her father asked. "Don't tell me Shaw is playing at your heartstrings, trying to convince you to take him back."

Bea shook her head. "No, he's not. Because I didn't willingly leave him in the first place. That was your doing, you manipulative bastard."

Fenwick's head snapped back and he sucked in a breath. "Now, see here—"

"Let me guess," she interrupted. "All the letters

I wrote to Micah never actually made it to the post office, did they?"

Her father's face had grown red and he didn't respond. But he didn't need to. Bea recalled all too well the silver tray in the foyer where the family had placed outgoing mail. She shook her head, realizing how naive she'd been to trust that her letters had been dropped in the mailbox. Had her father combed through the mail himself, or had he entrusted one of the staff with the distasteful job of extracting her letters before they were sent off?

She stared at the man in front of her, her heart breaking anew as all her childhood illusions shattered into pieces. It was one thing to realize her father was human, with his own foibles and faults. It was quite another to know he had deliberately sabotaged her life, imposing his values over her choices. He'd resorted to lying because he'd known Bea had made up her mind about Micah. And he hadn't cared. Her father, the man who was supposed to value her happiness above all things, had purposefully broken her heart because she hadn't toed the line like a dutiful daughter.

"You disgust me," she said softly. Fenwick continued to sputter, but she rounded on her heel and headed for the door.

"Come back here!" he shouted. "I'm not through with you yet!"

She paused, her hand on the knob. "I'm done with you," she said firmly. "As of this moment, I no longer consider myself your daughter. Don't try to contact me—I won't respond." She yanked open the door and walked into the foyer, closing the door on Fenwick's answering bellow. With a nod at the secretary, Bea strode to the elevators, her head held high. The security guard scampered after her, jumping into the elevator just as the doors closed.

She felt strangely light, almost as if the argument had hollowed out her insides, draining her emotions and leaving nothing but empty space behind. It was an odd sensation, and for a moment Bea wondered if she was simply numb. Perhaps the regret and pain would hit later, after the enormity of what she'd done had sunk in.

I'm sorry, Micah. I tried.

She left the building and stepped into the sun, turning her face up toward the warmth. It really was a beautiful day, too pretty to spend indoors. There was a coffee shop across the street with several empty tables on the patio. The scene was too enticing to pass up, and a few minutes later, Bea sat in one of the black metal café chairs sipping a latte and enjoying the warm spring breeze.

Her emotions began to return, like new flowers opening their petals to the world. She waited, expecting a painful blow. But it never came. Instead, her chest filled with happiness as she imagined her life stretching out before her like a smooth, even path. Gone were the brambles and weeds of her worries and hurts, the shadowy overgrowth of her father's attempts to control her. The road ahead was clear and filled with promise, and she had Micah to walk beside her again.

She smiled into her cup, feeling luckier than any woman had a right to be. They would face difficulties, she knew. Life was far from perfect. But as long as she and Micah were together, Bea felt like they could take on the world.

She couldn't wait to get started.

Micah watched Bea enter the building and saw the security guard greet her. Satisfied she was as safe as possible under the circumstances, he pulled away from Colton Energy, resisting the temptation to circle the block and park in front of the building again. He knew Bea was more than capable of standing up to her father, but he hated the idea of her confronting him alone. Still, he had to respect her wishes in this, and it was probably for the best. Micah's presence would only anger her father, making it impossible for them to have a conversation.

"What do you say we get a little work done?" he asked Chunk. He needed to talk to Joey's fiancée, Angelina Cooper. From his search yesterday, he knew she lived in an apartment complex nearby. Hopefully she was home and he could interview her before Bea finished talking to her father. He didn't think Angelina would have much information regarding Joey's murder, but it wouldn't hurt to hear her take on things and find out if Joey had any enemies who might wish him harm. The police had spoken to her soon after discovering Joey's body, but Micah wanted to talk to her personally. As an added bonus, talking to Angelina would occupy his thoughts and keep him from worrying about Bea until she called.

A few minutes later, he parked in front of a strip of apartments in the older part of Red Ridge. The building showed signs of wear and tear, and the small yard in front held more weeds than flowers. He glanced around the lot, noting the preponderance of older-model cars, many of them sporting rust and damage from past accidents. It all painted a picture of a lower-middle-class neighborhood, and Micah wondered if Angelina had money troubles that had extended to Joey.

He clipped the leash to Chunk's collar and helped the dog out of the truck. Normally, Chunk wore a vest that identified him as a police dog, but Micah decided to leave it off so that they didn't look so official. Although Chunk wasn't trained as a therapy dog, Micah had found that sometimes the mere presence of the animal was enough to help witnesses relax as they told their stories. Hopefully he would have the same effect on Angelina.

They took the stairs to the second floor and set off down the hall. A faded welcome mat sat in front of Angelina's door, the once-colorful floral pattern now muted shades of brown and gray. Micah gingerly used the scratched brass knocker, half expecting it to come off in his hand.

He heard footsteps from within the apartment, then a pause as Angelina likely looked through the peephole. There was the rattle of a safety chain and then the door was pulled open a crack. "Yeah?"

Micah smiled at the woman. "My name is Micah Shaw. I'm with the Red Ridge police department." He showed her his badge, then clipped it back onto his belt. "I'm investigating the murder of Joey Mc-Burn, and I was hoping to talk to his fiancée, Angelina Cooper."

The woman shifted, her wary expression softening. "That's me."

"May I come in?"

She eyed Chunk. "You brought your dog?"

"In a manner of speaking. He's my partner."

She smiled faintly. "That's cool. I have a cat, though…" She trailed off, her doubt clear.

"Chunk is a perfect gentleman," Micah said. "He won't bother your cat at all."

"If you're sure…" She stepped back and pulled the door open wide, gesturing for them to come inside.

Micah glanced around as Angelina locked up behind them. Chunk vigorously sniffed at her legs, and to Micah's shock, the dog let out a low growl that he felt more than heard. He frowned, then saw the white cat at the end of the hall, who sat idly licking a paw. The cat spied Chunk and froze, his tongue still extended. Micah tightened his grip on Chunk's leash, hoping the dog wouldn't make a liar out of him. Normally, he was pretty calm around other animals, but there was always a first time…

Chunk sniffed the air, but otherwise didn't acknowledge the cat. His growl subsided, but the tension in his muscles remained. What was going on with him?

"It's okay, Casper," Angelina said soothingly. "The puppy isn't going to bother you."

The cat didn't seem impressed by his mistress's assurance. He took one last look at Chunk and sprinted away, presumably to the safety of the bedroom. Chunk sniffed again, but otherwise didn't respond to the feline's hasty retreat.

Angelina breathed out a sigh of relief, and Micah relaxed his hold on the leash. "We can talk in here," she said, leading him down the hall and into the living room. She took a seat on the couch and Micah settled into a nearby recliner, Chunk sitting stiffly at his feet. He placed a hand on Chunk's head, hoping to convince him to relax. He made a mental note to increase the dog's exposure to cats...

Her apartment was small but clean, the furniture on the older side with mismatched upholstery and spots of wear. Probably hand-me-downs from relatives or friends. Still, it was clear Angelina had worked to give the place a homey feel despite limited resources.

"How are you holding up?" Micah asked. He noted a small pile of crumpled tissues on the side table, next to an empty wine glass. He hadn't smelled alcohol on her as he'd walked past, so the glass was probably from last night. Maybe the wine had given her a few moments of peace.

Angelina shrugged, the motion jerky. "Okay, I guess. I've never lost anyone before. I don't really know how to handle this." Tears welled in her eyes, but she kept her head high. Micah leaned over and grabbed the box of tissues off the table, extending them toward her. She pulled out a few and dabbed at her eyes. "Thanks," she said.

"No problem." He shifted in the chair, trying to decide the best approach for this conversation. Talking to the families of victims was never easy, and he had to walk a fine line. If he was too sympathetic, Angelina would end up crying on his shoulder. But if he was too by-the-book, she might be put off by his formality and shut down. Either way, he wouldn't get the answers he needed.

In the end, he tried to strike a balance. "I know this is hard for you," he said. "But I need to ask you some questions about Joey and your life with him. Do you think you feel up to talking with me now?"

She nodded. "Might as well. I don't have anything else to do today."

"Is it your day off?"

She sniffed. "They gave me the week after they heard about Joey."

"Who's 'they'?" Micah retrieved the small notebook he kept in his pocket and flipped to a blank page.

"I work at The Ranch House," she said, naming the ritzy steak restaurant located in the well-to-do part of Red Ridge. "That's actually how I met Joey. I waited on his table one night, and he came back the next day. He asked me out, but I said no. I had dated a customer before, and it didn't go well. But Joey was persistent.

He ate there every night for a week until I agreed to give him a shot." She smiled at the memory and Micah nodded encouragingly. It sounded like Joey was a bit of a creep, but he wasn't about to say that to Angelina.

"Do you know if anyone was upset with Joey for any reason? Someone from his work, or maybe he had a falling-out with a friend?" Micah already knew Joey had worked as a surgical tech at the local hospital. He'd spoken with Joey's boss but hadn't gotten any leads from that conversation.

Angelina shook her head. "No. Everyone loved Joey."

"Everyone?" In Micah's experience, no one was universally loved. Even the most saint-like person was disliked by someone. It was just a matter of finding out who. And from what he'd gleaned in his investigation, Joey was a bit of a blowhard. A nice guy, by all accounts, but one with a loud mouth and a tendency to brag. His murder matched the MO of the Groom Killer, but maybe Joey's murderer had just made it look that way to throw off police. Had he picked a fight with the wrong guy?

Angelina frowned. "He got on some people's nerves, sometimes. But it was never anything serious. No one wanted to hurt him."

Micah decided to try a different tack. "I understand he proposed fairly recently?"

Angelina nodded and glanced down at the modest ring on her left hand. "Yes. About six weeks ago."

"Was he worried at all about the Groom Killer? A lot of people are hiding their engagements or even postponing them out of fear."

"No way." Angelina shook her head firmly. "Joey said he wasn't going to let some faceless bogeyman scare him out of marrying me. I told him I was fine with waiting, but he wouldn't hear it. He stood up in the middle of the Pour House and announced to everyone that he loved me and that we were getting married, and anyone who didn't like it could shove it."

"When was this?" Micah asked, taking notes.

"About a week ago." Angelina was quiet a moment, then sniffed. "Do you think the killer was in the bar that night?"

Micah tilted his head to the side. "It's possible." There was no evidence that Demi Colton had been hiding in the area a week ago, but it's possible she'd gone to the Pour House in disguise or had a friend who had heard Joey's declaration and told her about it. Joey had practically dared the killer to come after him, which made him an especially attractive target. Had his public announcement of love painted a bull's-eye on his back?

"What about you?" he asked. "Do you have any ex-boyfriends or anyone in your life that might be jealous of your relationship with Joey?"

She was quiet for a moment. "I don't think so. I didn't date much, and the men I did go out with never really stuck around long."

"Who was your last boyfriend? I might need to talk to him, just to rule some things out."

"Evan Larson."

Micah froze, the tip of his pen poised just above the paper. "Say again?"

"Evan Larson." Angelina wrinkled her nose. "He's handsome and rich, but he's also a jerk. I met him when I waited on his table—he was the first customer I went out with."

"I see. And how long did you see him?"

"Only a couple of weeks. Like I said, he's not that great of a guy."

"Did things end badly between you two?" If Larson still pined over Angelina, perhaps he had killed Joey or paid someone else to do it. Micah's heart began to pound with adrenaline. This might be just the break he needed to finally nab one of the Larson twins!

"Not especially," Angelina said. "He pitched a fit when I told him I wasn't interested in seeing him anymore. I don't think he's used to hearing the word *no*. But I walked away and he hasn't bothered me since."

That didn't sound like Larson. He wasn't one to take defeat easily, and Micah had to wonder if Evan had truly given up or was simply pretending to accept Angelina's wishes. Now that Joey was dead, would Evan try to position himself as a shoulder to cry on so he could win her back?

His phone buzzed in his pocket, and he pulled it out to read the text.

I'm ready. B

He typed out a quick reply and glanced at Angelina. "I'm sorry, but I have to go. Thank you for speaking with me."

She nodded and rose. "I just hope I was able to help."

"You did," Micah assured her. He retrieved one of his cards and passed it to her. "If you can think of anything else, or if Evan tries to contact you, please let me know."

"Evan?" She sounded surprised. "Why do you think he would want to talk to me?"

Micah shrugged. "Call it a hunch. Now that you're single, he might come knocking on your door."

Angelina studied his card before placing it on the end table, next to her pile of tissues. "I doubt it, but I'll let you know."

She led them to the door, unlocking it so he and Chunk could leave. "Please let me know when you find out who did this," she said quietly. She gripped the edge of the door, her eyes shiny with fresh tears. "It's only been two days, but I miss him so much already."

Micah's heart went out to the woman. The grief he'd experienced when he thought he'd lost Bea had been almost unbearable. He couldn't imagine how much worse it would be to know she was dead and he would never see her again.

He placed his hand on Angelina's upper arm, patting her gently. "We're working around the clock," he said. "We'll find the killer and make sure he pays for what he did to Joey."

She nodded, her lips pressed together to form a thin line. "In the meantime," he said, pausing in the hall. "Call me if you need anything."

"Thank you," she replied, her voice barely above a whisper. She closed the door behind him, and he heard a *snick* as she flipped the locks back into place.

"Come on, partner," he said to Chunk, tugging gently on the leash. They walked down the hall together and carefully navigated the stairs. Micah was still reeling at the revelation that Angelina had once dated Evan Larson, and he made a mental note to share that detail with the rest of the team as soon as possible. None of them had suspected the Larson brothers in the Groom Killer case, but perhaps they needed to reevaluate the evidence. Or maybe Larson had simply used the Groom Killer as a cover, staging Joey's murder to throw suspicion off himself?

Anything was possible.

Micah helped Chunk into the backseat and climbed behind the wheel. His thoughts turned to Bea, and a sense of anticipation fizzed in his system, chasing away the vestiges of Angelina's sadness that had followed him to the car. He felt sorry for the woman, but the best thing he could do for her was to catch the person who had killed Joey.

First, though, he had to pick up Bea.

He wasn't used to splitting his priorities between his personal and professional life. For so long, he'd been focused solely on his job to the exclusion of anything else. But now that Bea was back, he couldn't ignore the needs of his heart any longer.

The timing wasn't ideal. He felt a little guilty because he was no longer giving the Groom Killer case his full attention. But he and Bea had already lost too many years. Micah wasn't willing to pause the re-building of their relationship for even a second longer than necessary. Maybe he was just being selfish, but he couldn't bring himself to care. For the first time in a long time, he was going to put his own needs first.

He had definitely earned the privilege.

Chapter 12

"Are you sure you're okay?"

Bea smiled and reached over to touch Micah's arm, squeezing it gently in reassurance. "I'm fine," she said, repeating herself for the third time in ten minutes. It was sweet of him to worry, but she really was at peace with everything that had happened.

"You say that now, but…" He sounded doubtful, as if he expected her to suddenly change her mind and burst into tears.

"Micah, the man is toxic. He's not a father to me—he's a selfish jerk who thinks he can control everyone. His actions caused me years of pain, and what's more, he doesn't care. That's not something I'm willing to forgive or forget."

"I know," Micah said. But he didn't sound convinced.

Bea suspected there was something else bothering him. "What's really going on here?"

Micah stopped at a red light, then turned to face her. "I know your father isn't a nice man. But I don't want to come between you and your family. I don't want you to feel like you need to defend me against them or that you have to pick sides."

"I don't," she said simply. "Fenwick is the only one who has an issue with us being together, and that's his problem to deal with, not mine. My siblings don't care, and even if they did, this is my life. I'm not going to live it on someone else's terms."

Micah studied her, his green eyes warming. "Okay," he said, nodding slightly. "I trust you know your own mind on this. But promise me this—if things change and you decide you want a relationship with your father again, go for it. Don't hesitate because you think it would hurt my feelings or make me upset."

"All right." That was an easy enough request.

The car behind them honked, making them both jump. She glanced out the windshield to find the light had turned green while they were talking. Micah turned his attention back to driving, steering them toward police headquarters.

"Why are you so worried about my interactions with him?" she asked. Given what her father had done to them both, she wanted to understand why Micah was so insistent she try to preserve a relationship with the man. He had just as much right to be angry with Fenwick, and yet he seemed more concerned with their father–daughter connection than his own emotions.

Micah let out a soft sigh. He didn't respond right away, making Bea wonder if he'd heard the question. When he did speak, his voice was subdued.

"You know what my dad was like," he said. "His only love was the bottle, which made things…difficult at home."

Bea knew bits and pieces of what Micah's life had been like when they were both in high school. But he'd always been careful to shield her from his father, never letting her meet him and making sure she never came to his house. Bea had thought he was simply ashamed of his dad—the man's reputation was well known in Red Ridge—but now she wondered if there had been another reason for Micah's actions.

Her stomach lurched as her thoughts turned in a dark direction. "Did he hurt you?" she whispered.

Micah shook his head, and she breathed out a sigh of relief. "Not physically," he said. "But he was a mean drunk, and he lashed out at me and Mom a lot. And once Mom was gone…" He trailed off, and Bea's heart broke as she filled in the details.

"I'm so sorry," she said. "I wish I had known. Why didn't you tell me?" She and Micah hadn't been together when his mother had died—they'd started dating soon after—but he'd never given any indication of his troubles at home.

He swallowed hard, his Adam's apple bobbing in

his throat. "I didn't want the things that happened at home to touch you. I wanted to have one thing in my life that was pure and untainted by my dad. You were my sanctuary. All you had to do was smile at me, and I forgot all about my father and the horrible things he said."

Bea blinked back tears. "Oh, Micah…"

"My only regret is that Mom didn't live to meet you. I know she would have loved you."

"If she was anything like your aunt, she must have been amazing."

"She was," he said, smiling briefly. "Anyway, I never had a father who was interested in me. Even though he has his faults, your dad was a part of your life. I'd have given almost anything to have that, and I don't want to you wake up one morning after he's gone and mourn the time you could have had with him."

Bea mulled over his words, surprised to find they made a certain amount of sense. Right now, her anger toward Fenwick was still paramount, but would that always be the case? Would she eventually come to consider him in a different light? She didn't think she could ever forget what he'd done, but maybe the passage of time would soften the sharp edges of her feelings.

Micah pulled into the parking lot at police headquarters and found a shady spot. He killed the engine and turned to face her as they unbuckled their seat belts. "I'll support you, no matter what you decide. I just want to make sure you've examined all the angles first. It's very satisfying to act out of anger, but that's not always the best choice."

She nodded, appreciating his perspective. "You're right. And while I can't imagine changing my mind right now, I'll try to stay open to the possibility that I'll feel different in the future."

"Thank you."

She leaned over and kissed him lightly on the mouth. "No, thank you. Having you around gives me balance."

"Balance, huh?" He grabbed her arm and pulled her forward suddenly, causing her to fall into his lap. "Seems like you still need a little work in that department."

Before she could respond, he framed her face with his hands and kissed her properly, his tongue dancing with hers in a way that sent shivers of pleasure down her spine. Bea threaded her hands through his thick hair and wriggled her way over the center console until she sat fully in his lap. She pressed her chest to his, loving the feel of his hard muscle against her curves.

One of Micah's hands left her face to trail down her side. His touch was light over the fabric of her shirt, but her nerve endings flared to life nonetheless. She shifted in his lap, seeking greater access to his body. He let out a low groan and pulled back, resting his forehead against hers.

"I didn't think that through," he said, his voice husky. "I only meant to tease you, leave you wanting more."

"That wasn't very nice of you," she replied, rocking forward a bit to move against the bulge in his pants. He gasped, then placed his hands on her hips to keep her from doing it again. She smiled down at him. "Payback," she whispered, her lips curving in a seductive smile.

"I suppose I deserve it," he said.

She decided to take pity on him and crawled back over the console to the passenger seat. "What's your plan now?"

Micah cleared his throat. "We, uh, we wait a few minutes and head inside. I talked to Joey's fiancée today and need to update the guys."

The reminder of Joey's murder snuffed out the last embers of Bea's desire. She smoothed her hand over her shirt and hair, making sure everything was back in place. "Did you learn anything useful?"

"Maybe," he replied. He rubbed his eyes with one hand, looking suddenly tired. "She didn't know of anyone who might want to hurt Joey, but I found out she used to date Evan Larson."

Bea frowned. She was slightly familiar with the Larson twins—they lived down the street from Fenwick—but she'd never actually met them. "I take it that's important?"

Micah nodded. "It could be. We've known for a while that the Larson brothers are dirty, but they're so slick we haven't been able to gather enough evidence to make any charges stick."

"Hmm…" She tilted her head to the side. "Do you think he might have killed Joey?"

"I don't know if Evan is stupid enough to do the job himself," Micah said. "But I wouldn't be surprised if he paid someone to do it. That seems more his style."

"So then, the Groom Killer isn't involved after all?" The possibility filled her with a mixture of relief and concern. If the Groom Killer hadn't been the one to assault her, then there was no need to worry that she was next on the list. But then, who had hurt her? And why?

"I'm not willing to say that yet. The MO was the same—shot in the chest, black cummerbund in the mouth, soon before the wedding. This whole Larson theory is still just conjecture, unless and until we find evidence suggesting otherwise. It's possible the Larson brothers are somehow tied to the Groom Killer cases, but I don't know for sure. We haven't really examined that angle in the investigation, so it's going to take a little digging to figure out if this is an actual lead or just a wild goose chase."

Bea shook her head. The whole thing sounded complicated and frustrating, and she didn't envy Micah his job. "I guess you need to get started. I'll camp out in the break room while you work."

"Thanks." He cast a sidelong look at her, his lips curving in a smile that was wicked and filled with promise. "Rain check?"

Her stomach fluttered with anticipation. "Definitely."

Micah caught sight of Brayden almost as soon as they walked into the squad room. "There you are!"

Brayden said. He hung up the phone he'd had to his ear. "I was getting ready to call you."

"What's up?" Micah's interest sharpened—he might not be the only one with news. Had there been a break in the case?

"Ballistics report just came back," Brayden said. He passed a file folder over and Micah glanced at it, not bothering to sit down. He was dimly aware of Bea and Chunk heading for the break room, but his focus was on the results of the forensic investigation.

"So, the same gun killed Joey and the witness who claimed to see Demi shoot a man in the alley," he said.

"Looks that way," Brayden confirmed.

Micah closed the folder and tapped the corner against his palm, gathering his thoughts. "No witnesses to the second murder or prints, though."

Brayden shook his head. "Just like the other crime scenes. Whoever the killer is, they know what they're doing."

Which made it hard to believe this was the work of Demi Colton. Micah knew the woman was clever—as a bounty hunter, she had to be—but being street-smart didn't necessarily translate into having the skills required to commit a string of murders without leaving behind any physical evidence—other than her necklace at the first crime scene. And that finding might not even be connected to the crime. Demi's dad owned the Pour House, so it was possible she'd lost the necklace in the parking lot some time before the killing.

Chief Finn walked over to the pair of them. "Same gun?"

Micah nodded. The rest of the team gathered round, drifting closer to hear the latest. "Since everyone's here," Micah said, "I might as well fill you in on my progress." He told them about his conversation with Angelina and his suspicions regarding Evan Larson.

"We hadn't really considered the Teflon Twins as suspects," Finn said. "Maybe we should?"

Brayden nodded. "It's possible the other Groom Killer victims had ties to them, as well."

Micah shook his head. Finn noticed the gesture. "Something bothering you?" he asked.

"No." He shrugged. "Well, maybe. I'm just having trouble reconciling Joey's death with the other Groom Killer victims."

"Why's that?" Brayden asked.

"The whole thing feels staged to me. Why did the killer move Joey's body into the fitting room of Bea's shop? And since Tucker Frane suddenly reported seeing Demi kill a man near the bridal salon, then was killed that same night, by the same gun, it makes me think whoever did this was trying to tie up loose ends. Otherwise, why leave our first witness, Paulie Gaines, alive?" He ran a hand through his hair. "Maybe it's possible Tucker was paid to kill Joey, made up the story about Demi, and he was killed in turn to make sure he never revealed the truth."

The team was silent for a moment as each member considered his theory. "Why leave Bea alive, then?"

Shane asked. He glanced in the direction of the break room, the tips of his ears turning pink. "I mean," he said, lowering his voice. "She's kind of a witness, too. Why didn't Tucker just shoot her on his way out the door?"

That was the million-dollar question, the mystery that had kept Micah up late the past few nights. "From what we know about him, Tucker didn't seem to be the type of guy who improvised well. It's possible he saw her and panicked, and since he didn't have explicit instructions as to what to do, he hit her and fled."

"Most people shoot first and ask questions later," Shane pointed out.

"True," Micah acknowledged. "But if Tucker really was Joey's killer, he was paid to do it. He's not—or at least he wasn't—a killer by nature, so I don't think his first instinct would have been to kill someone else."

Carson shook his head. "I'm not buying it. Joey's murder fits with the Groom Killer's MO perfectly—shot through the heart, cummerbund stuffed in his mouth. We haven't released all those details to the public, so the only way someone could have made his death fit that pattern is if they killed the other victims, as well. That makes me think Joey is a true Groom Killer victim, not a staged murder."

There was a murmur of agreement from about half the team. But as Micah glanced around, he saw skepticism on the faces of several other officers.

"We still need to keep an open mind," Finn said.

"It's worth looking at the Larson twins, even if we only wind up ruling them out as suspects."

"When will the autopsy results on Frane come in?" Micah asked. "If he did kill Joey, there should be gunshot residue on his hands."

"Soon, I hope," Finn said. When Micah merely raised one eyebrow, Finn sighed. "I suppose you want me to call and light a fire under the coroner?"

"That'd be great, chief," he said, slapping the man on the back. "Thanks!"

Finn rolled his eyes and let out a long-suffering sigh. "You'd better hope he's in a good mood. I don't need an ass-chewing today."

"He likes you," Micah said with a smile. Finn shook his head. "Well, he likes you better than he likes me," Micah amended.

"I'll let you know what I hear," Finn said. "In the meantime, everyone, try to do a little digging into the Larson twins with an eye to seeing if they have any connections to our previous victims or witnesses."

There were nods all around as the group dispersed, leaving Micah and Brayden alone once again. "What do you think?" Micah asked, careful to keep his voice low.

Brayden shrugged. "It's definitely plausible," he said. "And it fits with the time line. Demi can't be in two places at once, and since that FBI agent is positive he saw her in Walker's Creek around the time of Joey's murder, she can't be his killer."

Micah nodded his agreement. "I think you're right."

Gratitude flashed in Brayden's eyes. Not for the

first time, Micah considered how difficult this case must be for his friend. "So, what do we do now?" Brayden asked.

"I'm going to take a drive out to Joey's house. His fiancée couldn't think of anyone who had trouble with him, but his neighbors may have seen a different side of things. It would be good to know if Joey had any drama at home he was keeping from Angelina."

Brayden nodded. "I'll keep digging into Frane's past, see if I can find a connection between him and the Larsons."

"Perfect. Call me if you need me."

"Likewise."

Micah walked back to the break room to find Bea making a list. "Doing okay?"

She glanced up with an absent smile. "Yeah. Just keeping myself busy while you work."

"What are you working on?" It was a nosy question, but he was curious to know what was occupying her thoughts.

She sighed. "Brainstorming, mostly. Trying to come up with ideas to keep my business afloat until you guys catch the Groom Killer."

A pang of sympathy made his heart flip-flop. "Any luck?"

Her shrug was answer enough. "Nothing that won't cost money in the short term. And that's kind of the problem. I don't exactly have a pile of cash lying around."

Micah wished he could help her, but he wasn't exactly flush himself. Still, he did have a little bit saved… "I'll give you what I have," he offered. He knew Bea wouldn't waste the funds or spend them on frivolous things. And if his modest nest egg was enough to keep her business afloat, he'd consider it money well spent.

"No," she said immediately. She shook her head to punctuate her response. "I love you for offering, but I can't do that."

His heart thumped at her use of the word *love*, even though she'd meant it in a casual way. "I admire your independence," he said with a smile. "Just know that my offer stands. If things take a turn, say the word and the money is yours."

Her eyes softened as she stared up at him. "Thank you," she said quietly. "It means a lot to know you'd trust me, and that you believe in me enough to do that."

"Of course." He leaned down, wanting to kiss her. Then he remembered where he was and drew up short. "Uh…" He cleared his throat. "Want to take a field trip with me?"

Bea gave him a knowing smile. "Sounds good," she said, grabbing her bag as she stood. "Where are we going?"

"Joey McBurn's house. I want to talk to his neighbors, see if they noticed anything unusual about the activity at his house. They were interviewed soon after the crime, but sometimes people remember things after a few days have passed."

"And you're letting me come with you?" She sounded surprised but happy.

"Yeah. I could use the company." It wasn't standard procedure to take a civilian along during a neighborhood canvass, but Micah didn't want to be away from her. Now that they had cleared the air between them, he wanted to spend as much time with her as possible. And he was still her bodyguard, regardless of this new turn in their personal relationship. Besides, having a woman with him might make people more willing to talk to him.

At this point, he'd take whatever advantage he could get.

Chapter 13

Joey McBurn had lived in an older neighborhood on the outskirts of Red Ridge. Bea eyed the houses as they drove by—they were on the small side, but most had tidy front yards.

It was easy to spot Joey's house; the grass was longer compared to the neighbors on either side, and a pile of uncollected newspapers sat in the yard. Even though Joey had only been dead a few days, the home had taken on an air of neglect. Bea shook her head as she climbed out of the SUV. "What a shame," she muttered.

She rounded the vehicle to find Micah attending to Chunk. The dog waited patiently while Micah wrapped him in a dark blue vest sporting the word POLICE in large white letters.

"I didn't know he had a uniform," Bea said.

"Oh, yeah," Micah responded. "It's important to make sure people know he's an officer and not just a pet. Helps cut down on misunderstandings, especially in a place like this, where other dogs might be around."

He clipped the leash to Chunk's harness and helped him out of the backseat. As soon as his paws hit the pavement, Chunk dropped his nose to the ground and began to sniff vigorously.

Micah tried to walk toward the closest neighbor's house, but Chunk tugged against his leash. Bea frowned; the dog was normally easygoing and well-behaved. It wasn't like him to resist a signal from Micah.

Micah noticed it, too. "What is it, boy?" Chunk pulled again, his nose still glued to the ground.

"Has he found something?" Bea asked, half afraid of what Micah would say. She remembered their earlier conversation, when he'd told her Chunk's specialty was cadaver detection.

"Possibly. No one thought to bring a dog out here during the first search of the house." He gave Chunk some slack on the leash, and the dog sniffed his way across the grass, headed for the gate that led to the backyard.

Micah opened the gate and Chunk darted inside. Bea followed behind them, a little worried at what they might find.

She let out her breath in a sigh of relief when she saw unbroken lawn in the back of the house. Everything looked normal to her eyes, but Chunk walked directly over to a patch of grass in the middle of the yard and sat. He glanced up at Micah expectantly, letting out a low *woof.*

Micah frowned as he studied the grass. "You sure?"

Chunk snorted, as if he was offended by the question. "Okay, buddy. You know I had to check." Micah began to circle around the spot, studying it closely. He stopped, crouching down with a nod. "I'll be damned," he muttered.

"What?" Bea asked.

"This is a new patch of grass," he said, not bothering to look up. "It looks like this whole section here—" he gestured with his arm "—is new."

"How can you tell?" She moved closer, trying to see what he saw.

Micah pointed to a spot. "The seam is there. It's barely visible, but it's there. And if you look closely, this section is just a little shorter than the rest of the yard."

It took her a second, but finally Bea saw the signs. "Oh." If Chunk hadn't led them to it, she never would have noticed the difference. Micah probably wouldn't have, either.

"Good job, Chunk." He pulled a treat from his pocket and gave it to his partner, then said, "Relax."

The dog's posture immediately changed, the tension leaving his muscles as he enjoyed his treat. Micah pulled his phone from his pocket.

"I thought he only detected blood?" Bea asked.

"He does," Micah replied absently, punching numbers on his phone.

"I don't see any here."

"That's because it's not here." Micah held the phone to his ear. "It's buried." Someone picked up on the other end of the line and Micah began talking, issuing a rapid stream of instructions and requests.

Bea knelt next to Chunk and scratched behind his ears. He closed his eyes in pleasure, his tail thumping against the grass. "I suppose congratulations are in order?" Chunk didn't respond, but when she stopped petting him, he nosed her hand in a silent request for more.

After a few minutes, Micah wrapped up his call. He squatted next to them, his gaze still on the patch of grass. "What happens now?" Bea asked.

"We wait."

It didn't take long for the forensics team from the county office to arrive, and soon the small yard was filled with people. Bea wandered off to sit on the porch steps, Chunk by her side. Micah wished he could talk to her, but there simply wasn't time.

The ground-penetrating radar showed signs of something buried under the grass. "Looks like at least one, maybe two bodies," the tech confirmed, his tone grim. "We'll start digging, see what we find."

They put up a portable awning to shield the spot from view, so anyone looking into the backyard from above—like the next-door neighbors, whose faces were already pressed against the glass of their second-story window—wouldn't be able to see anything. Then the team began to dig, carefully moving the grass and dirt, checking for any signs of evidence as they worked.

Brayden showed up just as the process got started. "How come you get all the excitement? I thought you were just coming out here to talk to people."

"So did I," Micah said, shaking his head. "You can blame Chunk for this one. If it hadn't been for his insistence, we never would have come into the backyard."

The pair watched the team work in silence for a few minutes. "You think it's human remains? Maybe he buried a dog not too long ago."

Micah cast him a sidelong glance. "You know Chunk only alerts for human blood."

"Yeah. I guess I'm just holding out hope. We've already had two murders in the past week alone. Any more and I'm going to feel downright unsafe." He grinned, but his point wasn't lost on Micah. The town of Red Ridge was already on edge thanks to the Groom Killer. If many more bodies turned up, people might start to panic.

"Want to do me a favor?"

"Sure," Brayden replied easily.

Micah nodded at the house next door. "They have a pretty good vantage point of this yard from that second-floor window. Care to knock on their door and see if they've noticed anything going on lately?"

"You think they're home?"

"Yeah. They were watching the show earlier. I'm

surprised they haven't come over to try to catch a better glimpse of things. They're probably dying to know what's happening back here."

Brayden gave him a knowing smile. "I'll be happy to fill them in."

"Use your judgment," Micah said as his friend walked away. He knew Brayden wouldn't tell the neighbors anything to jeopardize the investigation. But sometimes you had to give a little to get people to talk. If Brayden told them just enough to satisfy their curiosity, he might get a windfall of information in return.

Micah hoped so, anyway.

Just as Brayden left the yard, one of the techs stopped. "Officer? We've got something here."

Micah walked over to the edge of the dig site and crouched down, peering into the dirt. A hand had been exposed, ghostly white against the dark brown of the earth.

"There's one on this side, too," called the other man.

Micah walked around the perimeter of the site to see a torso had been uncovered, still clothed in a plaid flannel shirt. He nodded, grimly satisfied by their discoveries. "So, two bodies, then. Any signs of more?"

"Not right now," replied the first tech. "It's possible there are more, but the radar is usually pretty accurate."

"How long until you'll have them out?"

"Not long," the tech said. "We'll move a little slower now, but the dirt is nice and loose, and these bodies still look fairly fresh. Shouldn't take more than a half hour or so."

"Thanks," Micah said. "I'll leave you to it. Let me know when you've got their faces exposed, yeah?"

The two men nodded and Micah reached for his phone again. Finn had asked for updates as soon as he knew anything, and this was definitely information worth passing along.

"We've got at least two, chief," he confirmed.

Finn swore softly. "Any signs of trauma?"

"Not yet," Micah said. "But the team said it won't take long to fully exhume the bodies."

"This is definitely not the Groom Killer's style."

"I agree," Micah said. "I think we have to assume this is the work of someone else."

"Wonderful." Finn's voice practically dripped with sarcasm. "That means we now have at least two killers at large in Red Ridge."

"I'm afraid so," Micah said.

"Why Joey's backyard?" The chief's tone was thoughtful. "Do you think he killed them? Or is this just a strange coincidence?"

"I don't know," Micah admitted. "As soon as we can identify the bodies, I'll start looking for any connections to Joey. But my gut instinct is to say he didn't kill them. I don't think they've been in the ground that long—it's quite possible they were killed after Joey's murder and dumped here because this is the last place anyone would look for them. Not many people would think to explore a dead man's backyard, and it looked like whoever did this took pains to try to blend in the dump site with the rest of the yard."

"So this probably wasn't meant to send a message."

"No." If the killer had wanted the bodies to be found, they wouldn't have gone to the trouble to camouflage the burial location. "I think these people were meant to disappear without a trace."

"If that's the case, maybe we'll get lucky on the evidence front. If the murderer thought his victims would never be discovered, perhaps they got a little sloppy and left something behind for us."

"I've got my fingers crossed," Micah said.

"Keep me posted," Finn said. He ended the call and Micah stuck his phone back into his pocket.

Bea and Chunk were still sitting on the steps of the back porch. He wandered over and sat next to her, offering what he hoped was a reassuring smile. "How are you doing?"

Her hazel eyes were wide as she watched the team work. "I'm okay," she said. "I just never expected anything like this to happen. When you said we were going to talk to the neighbors, I figured that was that. I had no idea Chunk would…" She trailed off, swallowing hard. "Uh, find something."

"Me, neither," he confirmed. "Usually, I give him a signal to start searching. But I guess the smell was so strong, he couldn't ignore it."

Bea glanced over at the dog, who was placidly watching the activity in the yard. "He's really impressive. And the way he told you he'd found something—

I thought he'd start barking or digging at the ground. But he just sat down with a quiet woof."

Micah smiled at his partner. "That's what he's trained to do. It's important he not disturb the site, since it might contaminate or even destroy important evidence if he started pawing around. And most working dogs are trained to give a subtle signal rather than raise a ruckus."

"Why is that?"

Micah shrugged, searching for an answer. "I think, in most cases, it's best if the dog remains calm. If you're talking about a dog that detects explosives or something dangerous like that, you don't want his tell to set things off or make the situation more volatile."

"That makes sense," Bea murmured. "Was Duke a lot like Chunk?"

"Ah, no." Micah chuckled at the thought. "Duke was a high-strung dog. I think *perfectionist* is the best way to describe him. He was always alert, ready for anything."

"What was his specialty?"

"Explosives. He was trained to detect munitions and roadside bombs, that kind of thing. He saved a lot of lives, and the team held him in high regard."

"I'm sure they did," Bea said. "Do you know how he's doing now?"

"He's good. I actually got an email the other day from the nurse who adopted him. He's adjusted well to civilian life, and she told me he's been in some tracking competitions."

"I guess you can take the dog out of the army, but you can't take the army out of the dog?"

"Pretty much," Micah said. "It can be hard for these animals to retire. I'm glad she's keeping Duke occupied. It sounds like he's happy."

"Do you wish you had adopted him?"

Micah considered the question and the mixed feelings it triggered. He did miss Duke, but he knew he wouldn't have been able to provide the best life for him. "Sometimes. But I don't think it would have been fair to him, in the end. He wouldn't have liked staying at home while Chunk and I worked. It's better for him to be with her—he's her only dog, and she can devote all her time to him, which is what he needs."

"It must have been hard to give him up, though," she said quietly.

The memory of their goodbye put a lump in Micah's throat. "It was," he confirmed. "The only reason I was able to do it was because I saw how much she cared about him and how attached he'd grown to her during his time in the hospital."

"He sounds like quite a dog."

"One of the best," Micah said simply. "I've been thinking about taking a road trip to visit him, once this investigation is over. Maybe you could join me?"

She smiled. "I'd like that."

Warmth bloomed in Micah's chest. It felt so *normal* to sit next to Bea, chatting and making plans for their future. For a moment, it was like the last ten years had never happened, like they'd never been apart at all. If he closed his eyes, he could forget about the gruesome scene taking place before them and pretend they were sitting at the kitchen table, talking about a fun summer trip. He was excited at the thought of introducing Duke to Bea. He wanted her to have a connection to that part of his life, and if she met Duke, she'd have a better understanding of what his time in the Rangers had been like. Not all of it—he didn't want to share the horrible details of war with her. But he wouldn't mind talking to her about the lighter times, the moments of levity he'd had with Duke and his team. He hadn't had anyone to share that with since retiring from the army, and as time passed, he realized he wanted to talk about those memories as a way of keeping them alive.

"Officer?"

One of the techs was waving him over. Micah stood and crossed the yard in a few strides, arriving at the edge of the dig site. "We're about ready to remove this body," the man said, pointing into the hole they'd made. "Thought you might want to check him over now, so we can bag him before we put him on the gurney." He cast a meaningful look in Bea's direction, and Micah felt a flash of gratitude at the tech's thoughtfulness.

"I appreciate that," he said quietly.

He crouched at the edge of the makeshift grave to get a better look at the first body. "I'll be damned," he muttered to himself. A flash of excitement sent a tingle through his limbs as he stared down at the face of a man he'd seen just yesterday.

Thad Randall's body lay in the shallow grave, the

bullet hole in the center of his forehead a testament to how he'd died.

"Guess you won't be talking to Evan Larson anymore," Micah said. He straightened up and nodded at the men to proceed with their work. They carefully placed the body in a thick black bag and heaved it over the edge of the dig. A few minutes later, they'd uncovered the second body. Micah studied the man's face, but he didn't recognize him. No matter. The forensics team would go over the bodies with a fine-tooth comb, collecting evidence, fingerprints and DNA samples. If this man ran in the same circles as Thad Randall, he was probably already in the system. It was only a matter of time before they had a name to match the face.

"You need me to stay?" There was a marked police car out front with a uniformed officer to provide scene security, but Micah wanted to make sure the techs didn't need him for anything before he took off.

One of the techs shook his head. "We're almost done here. Once we get everything back to the lab we'll get started processing it all."

"Put a rush on it, please," Micah said. "These murders may be connected to the Groom Killer case."

"Will do."

Micah left the men to their work and punched out a quick text to Brayden before heading back to Bea. Her face was pale now, her mouth set in a pinched line. It was clear she was upset, and Micah figured it was time to go. Even though she hadn't actually seen the bodies, this situation had to be disturbing to her.

He was so used to death and ugliness he had forgotten what it was like to be innocent, and now he kicked himself for dragging her into this part of his world.

Reaching down, he took her hand and gently pulled her to her feet. He whistled for Chunk and together the three of them set off for his SUV. He couldn't change what she'd already seen, but he could try to distract her so she didn't think about it every time she closed her eyes.

And he knew just how to take her mind off things.

Chapter 14

Bea stared sightlessly out the window as Micah drove them back to the police station. He was on the phone most of the drive, talking to one of his fellow officers about the scene in Joey McBurn's yard. She tuned him out, not really enjoying the color commentary. Micah was trying to be discreet about the details, but somehow his use of dry, clinical terms just made her memories worse.

Even though she hadn't actually seen the bodies, she'd found the whole scene disturbing. The techs in their white coveralls, thick boots, hair nets and paper face masks were like something out of a movie. And the way they'd heaved the first body out of the pit up onto the level ground? She shuddered, recalling all too well the meaty thud that had sounded as the bag landed on the dirt. In a way, she wished she had seen more—that way her imagination wouldn't be torturing her now, coming up with ever more gruesome images that would surely haunt her dreams.

She turned to watch Micah as he drove. He seemed totally unaffected by what they'd just experienced. And why wouldn't he? He'd been a soldier before becoming a police officer. Surely he was no stranger to death and its many forms. Still, it bothered her a little to see him so unfazed. They'd just seen two bodies pulled out of the ground, two people whose lives had been cut tragically short. Did that mean nothing to him? Was he really that callous now? Or was he simply compartmentalizing things, turning off his emotions so he could respond in a professional manner? She made a mental note to ask him about it later; she didn't feel up to talking at the moment.

Micah drove past the police station, heading farther out of town. She frowned. "Where are we going?"

"I thought you might need a distraction," he said, casting a glance in her direction. A moment later, he turned into the parking lot for the K-9 training center. Her sister Patience worked here as a veterinarian, but Bea had never visited her at work before.

"So you brought me to see my sister?" It was a nice gesture, but Bea wasn't really in the right frame of mind to catch up with Patience. She'd much rather go home, brew a cup of tea and watch mindless television to take her thoughts off today's events. *No, not home*, she remembered sourly. She couldn't even do that anymore. The reminder made her already dark mood blacken further.

"Not exactly," Micah said. He climbed out of the truck and retrieved Chunk before walking over to her side of the vehicle.

"I don't understand," she said flatly. Whatever was going on here, she wished he would get to the point.

"I want to show you something."

Bea sighed. "I'm not really in the mood for surprises." She sounded bitchy even to her own ears, but recent events had taken a toll on her usual sunny outlook. After the break-in and her assault, and finding out her father had betrayed her and that Micah still had feelings for her, today's surprise exhumation was the icing on the cake of an emotional roller coaster. She needed to step off this ride from hell and center herself before the next blow that was sure to come.

Micah's green eyes were warm and understanding, as if he could tell she was at the end of her rope. "Five minutes. That's all I'm asking for."

She nodded. "Five minutes," she agreed. "Then you'll take me home?"

"If that's what you want."

Bea couldn't imagine why she wouldn't want to go home, but she let his comment slide. Together, the three of them walked into the training center and stopped at the front desk.

A young woman beamed up at them, her reddish-blond hair pulled into a serviceable ponytail. "Hey, Officer Shaw! Good to see you!" She stepped around the desk and knelt to lavish attention on Chunk. "And you, too, you pretty boy!"

Chunk sniffed and licked at the woman, clearly excited to see her. "How's it going, Danica?" Micah asked.

"Good, good," she replied, not bothering to look up. She only had eyes for Chunk, and the dog was eating up the attention. Bea had never seen his tail move that fast. "What brings you in today? I didn't see Chunk on the vet schedule. Is he doing okay?" Her voice changed, taking on a singsong quality as she addressed the dog directly. "Are you feeling all right, buddy? Do you need to see Dr. Patience?"

Micah smiled. "He's fine. I thought we'd stop in and take a look at the new recruits."

"Oh!" Danica popped back to her feet. "They're doing really well. I'd be happy to show you." She turned to Bea and stuck out her hand. "Sorry, I'm being rude. Danica Gage. I'm one of the trainers here."

"Bea Colton. Patience is my sister."

The woman studied her face, a smile blooming. "Yes, she definitely is. I can see the resemblance. Nice to meet you."

"You, as well," Bea said. She liked Danica already. There was something disarming about her obvious affection for Chunk, and Bea suspected he wasn't the only one to receive such an enthusiastic welcome.

"Right this way." Danica led them down a hallway, past several doors sporting large windows. Bea glanced in as they walked by, catching glimpses of kennels and what looked like dog supplies—food, toys, bedding and the like.

Danica made a few turns, then stopped in front of a door facing a bank of windows. A large, fenced-in yard was visible, and beyond that, Bea saw part of Black Hills Lake.

"Nice view," she remarked.

Danica turned to follow her glance. "Yeah. It really is pretty. Sometimes I have to tell myself to stop and enjoy the view. I get so caught up in work that I forget how nice it is."

Bea nodded, understanding perfectly. She was surrounded by beautiful gowns all day, every day. Each dress was a work of art, and yet she often found herself treating them as just another article of clothing. She handled them carefully, of course, but there were days she didn't really *see* them at all. Often, it took the exhilarated look of a bride who'd found her dream gown to help Bea appreciate the beauty again.

Danica peered through the window cut high in the door. "Okay, these guys are working on simple commands right now, but they're about due for a break." She knocked twice on the door and it was opened by another young woman. "Up for some visitors?"

"Sure thing," the second trainer replied. "We're wrapping up now."

Danica nodded and gestured for Bea and Micah to come inside.

Bea followed her into the room and gasped. Sitting in a row along the far wall was a line of puppies, each one wearing a mini harness like the one Chunk had been wearing earlier. There were five dogs in all, each one so adorable it nearly made her teeth hurt to look at them.

The dogs studied her, their eyes bright and interested as they watched Danica and Bea walk into the room. But when they saw Chunk they yipped in excitement and danced in place. A few piddled on the floor, and the second trainer moved quickly to mop up the messes.

For his part, Chunk let out a happy bark and made an elaborate bow to the puppies. Apparently interpreting this as some kind of signal, the dogs rushed at him en masse, circling and jumping on Chunk with abandon. Chunk sniffed at the newcomers and tolerated the attention with good grace. He pawed at the noses of a few of the bolder puppies, but his actions were gentle and the dogs were undeterred in their investigation. After a moment, Chunk rolled onto his back, his long ears spread out on the floor as the dogs scampered over and around him.

"Oh, my goodness," Bea whispered. "I've never seen anything so cute in my life!"

"Would you like to pet one?" Danica offered.

Bea started nodding before Danica had finished speaking. "If that's okay. I don't want to mess up their training. I know working dogs aren't supposed to be touched while they're on the job." She found a spot a few feet away and sat, unable to tear her gaze away from the scene before her.

"It's okay. They're on break now. Besides, thanks to Chunk, we'll never be able to get their attention again." She walked over and scooped up one of the quieter puppies and deposited the dog in Bea's lap.

Bea touched one velvet-soft ear with her fingertip, then the other. "Hello," she said quietly. "What's your name?"

"That's Zoe," Danica said. "She's a sweetheart."

Bea felt Micah settle on the floor next to her and lean close. "Pretty girl," he said, his voice soothing.

Zoe wriggled her little body, her tail going a mile a minute as she sniffed and licked Bea's hand. "What kind of dog is she? She looks like a German shepherd, but not quite."

"She's a Belgian Malinois," Danica replied.

"How old is she?"

"About nine months. Training doesn't officially begin until the dogs are around a year old, but we like to start early, acclimating them to the staff and the facility. We play with them and teach them simple commands, then work on building and expanding their skills as their attention span matures."

"They're all so cute." Zoe settled into her lap while another puppy wandered over to sniff Micah's shoes. He jumped back, startled, when Micah stretched out a hand to pet him. The dog sniffed cautiously, then allowed Micah to touch him.

"I'm not gonna hurt you, buddy," Micah said. He stroked the puppy's back with firm, even swipes of his hand. After a few seconds, the dog decided he liked the attention, after all, and his little body relaxed. Micah smiled. "He reminds me of Duke."

"He was suspicious of new people?" Bea asked.

Micah nodded. "Yeah. But once he knew you, everything was fine." He continued stroking the puppy, his expression thoughtful. "I like dogs that make you work for it a little bit. Feels like you've really earned something when you gain their trust."

"Chunk seems like an equal-opportunity kind of dog," Bea observed, watching as he interacted with the puppies. She'd never seen him so relaxed and playful before, and she imagined this was a nice break for him, too.

"Yeah, Chunk's a big softie," Micah confirmed. "But I don't hold it against him. He's actually pretty good about separating the good from the bad. In my experience, he's only affectionate toward people who are innocent or can be trusted. If we're around bad guys, he's very reserved and standoffish. He even snapped at someone once, when he thought they were trying to hurt me."

"Wow." She glanced at Chunk, who was lying on the ground, a look of total bliss on his face as one of the puppies chewed on his ear. "That's surprising."

"He's got his limits, just like we all do." Micah gave the puppy a final pat, then got to his feet. "I have to run back to the station for a bit. Would you like to stay here? I think you'll be safe with all the people around."

The thought of going back to the world of dead bodies and serial killers was unappealing, but she didn't want to wear out her welcome at the training center. "Only if it's okay," she said.

"Totally," Danica said. "You can help me feed these guys, if you want."

"Absolutely," Bea said, feeling a flash of gratitude at the woman's easy acceptance of her presence.

Micah nodded, a small smile playing at his lips. "I'll come back for you later. Call me if you need me." He called for Chunk and his partner got to his feet, albeit a little reluctantly.

"You can leave him, too," Danica said. "I'd be happy to look after him, as well."

Micah nodded. "If you're sure," he said. "I think he likes being around the little ones."

"It's good for them, too," Danica replied. "Gives them something to strive for."

Bea laughed at the absurd thought but she appreciated the sentiment.

"I'll try not to take too long." Micah offered her a final smile before turning to the door. She wanted to tell him not to worry about it—she knew he must have a lot of work to do, and she didn't want to keep him from it. But he was gone before she could say anything.

She felt an odd pang of longing at his absence. After spending so much time together over the last few days, she'd grown to take Micah's presence for granted. It was a little unsettling, how quickly she'd let him into her heart again.

A small voice in her head worried she was moving too fast, growing too emotionally dependent on Micah. But after so many years apart, could she afford to waste more time?

"Ready?"

She glanced over to find Danica holding clipping leashes on three of the puppies. "Ready for what?"

"Time to feed these guys, and then they'll need a potty break. Will you help me with that?"

"Sure thing." Bea got to her feet, and gestured to the other puppies still tussling with Chunk. "Should I take them?"

"Please."

She attached leashes to the other dogs, her focus immediately shifting from thoughts of Micah to keeping hold of the leads as the animals pulled and tugged in various directions. *Micah was right, after all*, she thought with a wry smile. *I'm not ready to go home yet.*

"Chief, I'm telling you, we need to bring Larson in right now for questioning."

Finn let out a long-suffering sigh and met Micah's stare. "And I'm telling you, we're not ready yet."

"We found Thad Randall's body in a shallow grave," Micah said. "The same Thad Randall I saw talking to Larson in the park yesterday morning." He waved his phone, the incriminating photographs displayed on the screen.

Finn lifted one brow. "I understand," he said, his tone curt. "But just because they spoke to each other doesn't mean Evan killed him. That's a big leap, and I'm not willing to drag Larson in for questioning until we've wrapped up our investigation into his connections to the Groom Killer victims."

"But, chief—"

"No, Shaw. These guys are slippery. If we tip our hand too early, they'll get away like they always do. We do this right. No jumping the gun. Give Carson and the rest of the team time to finish checking into things. Then we bring both twins in and hit them with everything we've got."

Micah knew Finn's approach made sense, but he still wasn't happy about the wait. His emotions must have shown on his face, because Finn gave him an understanding look.

"Go home, man. Try to get some rest. You've been burning the candle at both ends for months now. Take the night off and try to relax."

Micah huffed out a humorless laugh. "Sure thing, boss. I'll get right on that."

"You'd better try," Finn remarked. "I expect you back here first thing tomorrow morning with a new attitude."

Embarrassment flooded Micah's system, making his skin feel hot and tight. "Yes, sir," he said quietly. He deserved that remark, but it still stung.

Finn nodded and the tension in the room dropped a few notches. "We'll get these guys," he said softly. "Have a little faith."

Micah wished it were that simple. Still, he managed a nod and a small smile before leaving Finn's office.

Back at his own desk, he pondered his next move. A small, selfish part of him rejoiced at Finn's admonition to take the night off. That meant he could take

Bea home and enjoy the evening with her without feeling guilty about ignoring the case. It was a little surprising, the way he'd come to lean on her over the past few days. She was a calming force in his life, and when he was around her, he felt more at peace. Maybe he was making a mistake, relying on her when she had no idea of or control over her effect on him. They'd been apart for so long—if she decided she didn't like the man he'd become, would he be able to pick up the pieces and move on with his life? Or was he setting himself up for a huge fall?

Just the thought of losing Bea again made his chest ache, and he rubbed at his breastbone with a fist. *Don't think about it*, he told himself. But as a former soldier and a cop, he couldn't help but consider the worst-case scenario.

He turned to his computer, needing a distraction. He didn't want to pick up Bea quite yet—she'd seemed to be enjoying her time with the puppies, as he'd hoped she would. Given the events of the past few days, he wanted her to have a break, a little ray of sunshine to brighten her spirits. In the meantime, there was always work for him to do. He pulled up a blank form and began typing his report on today's exhumation. It was a tedious job, but Micah knew it was important. He wanted to make sure he'd dotted all the *i*'s and crossed all the *t*'s so when they brought the Larson twins in for questioning, their lawyer wouldn't find even the smallest technicality to use in their defense.

"I'm coming for you," he muttered. "And this time, you won't get away so easily."

It was over an hour before Micah finished the paperwork and went to pick up Bea. The sun hung low in the sky as they drove home. He hadn't been able to shake his bad mood yet, but he enjoyed listening to Bea talk about the puppies. Even Chunk seemed to be in a good mood, his tail thumping a quiet tattoo against the backseat.

"I'm glad you had a nice time," Micah said, pulling into the drive.

"I did," she said, a happy smile on her face. "I might even start volunteering there, just so I can spend more time with the dogs."

"I'm sure they'd appreciate that," Micah said. "I know they're always busy."

"Thank you," she said simply.

"For what?"

She waited until they were in the house before responding. "For taking me there today. It was exactly what I needed after this afternoon, but I didn't know it."

Micah brushed off her thanks as he gathered Chunk's bowl and kibble. "Dogs are pretty amazing creatures. There's a reason so many of them work in hospitals and rehab centers."

After feeding Chunk, Micah retrieved ingredients from the fridge and set about making sandwiches while Bea fixed a green salad. He slid the plate in front of her with an apologetic grimace.

"I know it's not fancy, but at least it's food."

"Looks fine to me."

They ate in silence for a few moments. Micah knew he wasn't being very good company, but he couldn't seem to shake his disappointment and anger over the pause in the investigation. It was only a slight delay, but given today's developments, he didn't want to wait to talk to Larson. He wanted to see the look on that bastard's face when he saw the pictures of Thad Randall's body...

"What's on your mind?" Bea's voice cut into his thoughts and he jumped a little.

"Hmm?" he replied absently.

"Something is obviously bothering you. What's going on?"

She looked genuinely interested, and for a moment, Micah was tempted to tell her everything. But she still had a glow about her from her time with the puppies, and he didn't want to bring down her mood with talk of the case.

He shook his head, hitting the reset button on his mood. "Just work stuff. I'm fine."

Bea's expression told him she wasn't buying it, but she didn't respond. After a moment, she spoke again. "I wish you had been able to stay a little longer at the training center. Chunk was really cute with the puppies. I think he fancies himself their big brother or something."

Micah smiled, imagining the scene easily. "He certainly has the right temperament for it. I was thinking about asking Danica and some of the other trainers

if Chunk could be helpful to them once he retires—
that way, he can still have a job without all the rigors
and pressures of police work."

Bea leaned over, glancing past him to the dog in
question, who was now snoozing peacefully on one of
the kitchen rugs. "He may surprise you. I know you
said working dogs tend to have a hard time adjusting to retirement, but I think Chunk might be equal
to the challenge."

Micah couldn't help but laugh at her assessment.
"You're probably right." Chunk was one of the more
laid-back dogs at the station, equally happy to go out
in the field on a search or snooze next to Micah's desk
while he completed paperwork. Compared to Duke's
Type-A, full-of-energy personality, Chunk was practically a Zen master.

They spent the rest of the meal chatting amiably
about safe topics. Bea told him about helping brides-
to-be find the perfect dress, and Micah told her more
about the police dog training process. He felt himself
relaxing, his frustrations and worries fading as he
learned more about Bea's life and shared some of his
own. It was like they were a normal couple, catching
each other up on the events of the day, rather than a
cop protecting the woman he'd loved and lost from
an unknown assailant who was likely connected to
a serial killer.

His heart lightened as he imagined many more
evenings like this, the two of them talking at the table
to the accompaniment of Chunk's soft snores. Even
though he couldn't see the solution now, he knew the

Groom Killer case wasn't going to last forever. At some point, the team would get a break and they'd catch the culprit. Then his life would return to normal, her business would recover, and he and Bea could focus on building their future without this gray cloud of uncertainty hanging over their heads.

It was a nice thought, and he wondered if she imagined the same thing. There was only one way to find out.

Gathering his courage, Micah took a deep breath. "I want to ask you something."

Bea stilled, her hand clutching her glass of water. "Oh?"

He was committed now. His stomach fluttered with nerves, but he had to know what she was thinking. If Bea didn't feel the same way, it was better for him to find out sooner rather than later. "Do you... how do you see things going in the future?"

"Between us?"

Micah nodded. "I know you had a tough conversation with your dad today. Now that you've had a little time to think about everything, are you still at peace with your decision where he's concerned?"

"Yes." She didn't hesitate, didn't sound uncertain at all. "I told you, Micah. I can't overlook the fact that he deliberately sabotaged our relationship and feels no remorse over hurting me. There is no room in my life for someone like that."

"Okay." Micah nodded, knowing it was time to let the subject go. As much as he hated the thought of Bea losing her father, he had to admit her reasoning made sense. If someone he cared about hurt him as badly as Fenwick had Bea, he didn't think he'd be able to forgive and forget, either.

Now he just had to hope that what she'd said earlier was true—that she wouldn't come to resent him for the way her relationship with Fenwick had ended.

"Is that what's bothering you? You're worried I'm going to have a change of heart?"

He jerked one shoulder up in a shrug. "That's part of it, yeah." How could he explain his fears without sounding totally pathetic? *You broke my heart once, and even though it wasn't your fault, I'm worried it's going to happen again because you regret picking me over your father.*

She studied him for a moment, her hazel eyes kind. "I chose you," she said softly. "And I will keep choosing you. I know this is still new between us, and I know we're both feeling our way back into being together again. But let's keep my father out of this. Even if you and I hadn't been interested in picking up where we'd left off, I still would have told him the same thing."

Her words dissolved the weight on his heart, and Micah smiled in relief as a sense of peace engulfed him.

Bea rose from her chair and moved toward him, her hips swaying as she closed the distance between them. Micah watched her walk, feeling truly relaxed for the first time in a long time.

She knelt before him, her blond hair framing her face as she stared up at him. His breath caught in his throat as he traced her features with his gaze: the arch of her brows, the line of her nose, the curve of her lips. Would he ever get used to the sight of this beautiful woman? He'd taken her presence for granted once before. He wouldn't make that mistake again.

Micah reached out and traced her cheekbone with the tip of his finger. She closed her eyes and sighed quietly, angling her head into his touch.

"It's been a long day," she said softly. "And a tough one, for a lot of reasons."

"Yeah."

"Let's go to bed. Forget about it all."

His heart tripped in his chest. Was she asking what he thought? Or was he misinterpreting her words, hearing what he wanted instead of what she was actually saying?

She stared up at him expectantly, and he realized she was waiting for him to respond. Oh, God. Talk about pressure. If she had meant "bed" as in sleep and he said the wrong thing, she might think he was only interested in sex. But if she was hoping to connect with him and he rejected her, she might pull back and decide not to risk her heart again.

This was too important to risk. So rather than pretend he understood perfectly, he decided to ask for clarification. Maybe she'd think he was dense, but it was a chance he was willing to take.

"When you say *bed*, what exactly do you mean?" He held his breath, feeling like he was in suspended animation as he waited for her reply.

The sly curve of her lips told him everything he

needed to know. She got to her feet and held out her hand. He took it, and she pulled him up.

"Come with me, and I'll show you."

Chapter 15

Bea led Micah down the hallway, her stomach dancing with nervous excitement and anticipation. They had both changed so much in the last ten years. Would this connection still feel as right, as perfect now as it once had?

She hesitated when they reached the doors to the bedrooms. Which one? Micah gently nudged her forward, past the guest room and toward the master suite. "Bigger bed," he said softly, his voice a low rumble that made her shiver.

A few more steps and they were inside his private space. Bea glanced around, curious to see where Micah slept. As he had said, a large bed dominated the room, the simple wooden headboard pressed against the far wall. A dark green bedspread was tossed haphazardly over the mattress, almost as an afterthought. A dresser stood on the opposite side of the room, between the doors for the closet and bathroom. It was sparsely decorated in terms of furniture, but the framed pictures on the walls were the real jewels.

Unable to help herself, Bea moved closer, wanting to see the details. All of the photos had been taken in the woods, and many of them showcased animals: a trio of fox kits playing next to a fallen log, a pair of deer nuzzling noses, a black bear stretching toward the sun.

"These are amazing," she said, moving from one photo to the next, marveling at Micah's talent.

"Thanks." His voice was close, making her jump. She'd been so distracted, she hadn't realized he'd moved to stand behind her.

He ran a soothing hand down her arm. "Didn't mean to startle you."

Bea turned to face him and rested her hands on his shoulders. "You have a real gift," she said. "Have you ever thought about selling some of your work?"

He chuckled and shook his head. "No."

"I doubt you'd have any problems finding buyers."

His expression turned thoughtful. "It's not about money for me. I do it because I love it. If I tried to sell the photos, I don't think I'd enjoy taking them as much."

"I can understand that. It's a shame though—I'd love to have some of these on display in the boutique."

The tips of his ears turned pink at the compliment. "Tell you what—when this is all over, we'll sit down and look through my collection. You can hang whatever you want in the shop."

She smiled, appreciating his compromise. "Deal." She rose to her tiptoes and kissed him softly to seal the arrangement.

His arms tightened around her waist and he lifted her, leaving her feet dangling a few inches off the ground. "Oh, good," he whispered against her mouth. "I was wondering if you'd changed your mind."

Bea hooked her ankles around his waist and nipped at his lower lip. "Not a chance."

Micah walked them over to the bed and gently lowered her until she was sitting on the mattress. He straightened, his fingers going to the buttons on his shirt.

She grabbed his hands, stilling them. "Let me?" It was part question, part plea. She wanted to be the one to undress him, to take her time exploring him, getting to know the man he'd become in the time they'd been apart.

He dropped his hands and nodded. "Only if you let me return the favor," he said.

Just the thought of Micah undressing her made her limbs tingle. A flare of heat bloomed in her chest, making her muscles feel pliable and melted. The promise in his voice was almost enough to convince her to rip the shirt off his body so he would touch her, but she checked the impulse. She wanted their reunion to be special, not a frantic coming together driven by instinct. There would be time for that later.

She got to her knees, the mattress putting her head

level with his shoulders. She felt his gaze on her as she reached for the first button, but she kept her focus on his shirt. If she met his eyes, it would be all too easy to fall into those green depths and forget what she was doing.

Her fingers trembled a little as she opened his shirt button by button, slowly revealing a growing expanse of skin. When she reached the end, she grabbed the now-loose fabric and slid it from his shoulders.

His chest was broad, wider than she remembered. More muscular, too. She traced the hard slopes and lines with the tip of her fingers, causing him to draw in his breath with a hiss. Goose bumps broke out across his skin in the wake of her touch, and his muscles tensed and jumped as she explored. Acting on impulse, she leaned forward to blow warm breath across his skin. He shifted, a low moan escaping his throat.

Bea smiled and continued, still refusing to look at his face. Red-gold hair dusted his chest, tapering down his torso to form a line that bisected his taut stomach. She ran her hand over it, shivering as she imagined the feel of it against her bare skin.

She took her time, exploring him at a leisurely pace. The Micah she had known was still there, the foundation of the man she saw before her now. In many ways, it was a relief to find him. Micah had been so good to her over the past few days, but she could tell he was holding something back. Getting to know his body in this way made her realize the young man she'd known was still there, that his core hadn't changed at all. It was only natural he'd be worried about this new beginning. Bea had told him repeatedly she still wanted him, that she wasn't going anywhere. But actions spoke louder than words. Hopefully she could convince him with her body that her love for him was still going strong.

It took a few seconds for her to unbuckle his belt and unfasten his pants. They dropped to the floor with a thud, leaving him in a pair of boxer-briefs that did nothing to disguise his arousal. Her mouth went dry as she took in the evidence of his desire, and she reached out to touch him.

Micah's hand grabbed hers before she could make contact. She glanced up to find him staring down at her, his eyes bright with a swirl of emotion. "Not yet," he said, his voice little more than a growl. "My turn first."

Bea nodded and dropped her arm, submitting to his request. Micah gave her shoulder a gentle shove, pushing her onto her back. He stepped between her legs, looming over her. His expression was a mixture of satisfaction and anticipation, and she got the impression he was going to pay her back for every touch, every tease she'd just administered to him.

Her skin felt tight, her nerves raw and exposed. Micah reached for her shirt, his fingers brushing her neck as he moved. It was just a graze of skin against skin, but it was enough to make her squirm.

Micah climbed on the bed, straddling her hips. He noticed her reaction, and his answering smile was wicked and full of promise.

"Oh, yes," he murmured. "I'm going to enjoy this."

* * *

Micah's muscles trembled with leashed energy as he carefully worked the buttons on Bea's blouse. Her exploration of his body had left him so aroused he could barely see straight, but his first glimpse of the creamy skin of her shoulders helped him focus.

She was lovely—that was the only word he could think of that did her justice. Bea had always been beautiful, but seeing her now with her blond hair fanned around her face and her pale skin flushed pink with need, she was breathtaking.

He pulled the edges of her blouse apart, baring her chest. Her bra was plain, a serviceable white cotton that screamed practicality. But on her it was transformed into one of the sexiest things he'd ever seen. Micah took a moment to simply stare, drinking in the sight of her. He'd never thought he'd see her this way again, and a rush of gratitude filled his chest, making it hard to breathe.

Bea wriggled underneath him. "Is everything okay?" She sounded a little self-conscious, and Micah realized she was worried about what he thought. He smiled down at her and ran his fingers along the edges of her bra straps. "Never better," he said softly.

She relaxed and he leaned forward to nuzzle the soft skin under her jaw. Her scent was intoxicating, the floral notes of her soap filling his nose in a potent bouquet that made his head spin. How he had missed this! Missed the feel of her, the warmth of her body next to his own. The sound of her breathing, the soft moans she made when he touched a particularly sensitive spot. It was everything he remembered, and so much more.

He took his time getting reacquainted, enjoying the new lushness of her curves and the gentle slopes of her body. She had filled out in all the right places since their last encounter, and the feel of her soft, smooth skin was nearly enough to push him over the edge.

Moving slowly, carefully, he removed her shirt and bra, then slid her pants off her hips and down her legs. Seeing her like this, exposed and vulnerable, made a lump of gratitude form in his throat. Bea was such a remarkable woman. He'd spent the last year of high school both amazed and humbled that she had chosen him out of all the other guys around. He'd figured he'd used up his lifetime allotment of luck then and there. But knowing that she wanted to be with him again, after so many misunderstandings and after so much time had passed made him figure someone must be looking out for him.

Not many people got a second chance in life. He wasn't about to waste this one.

He kissed her reverently, worshiping her with his lips and tongue. There were parts of his life he couldn't share with her, dark places he didn't want her to see. But here and now, he could show her how much he loved her.

He moved down her body, enjoying the sound of her soft moans as he touched and kissed her, re-learning her secret places. Finally, when he could stand it no longer, he reached over to the drawer and removed a condom.

He fumbled with the wrapper for a second, then frowned. "Damn," he muttered.

"What's wrong?" Bea's voice was so relaxed she sounded almost drugged.

"The condom is out of date." Disappointment was a heavy weight in his stomach as he hastily re-evaluated his plans. It would be all right, he decided. He could still make it good for her—

"It's okay," she said, reaching up to take the package from him. "I'm on the pill, and my most recent doctor's appointment didn't reveal any surprises."

"Me, too," he blurted. "Not the pill part, I mean. But I'm clean. And I haven't been with anyone in a really long time."

She smiled up at him, her eyes full of understanding. "Me, neither. No one ever measured up to you, so I kind of stopped looking."

Her words made his heart swell with love. "I know exactly what you mean." He leaned down and kissed her gently, once again humbled at the knowledge of her feelings for him.

Bea's fingers threaded through his hair, then moved down to graze lightly across the skin of his shoulders. Moving in unspoken agreement, they shed the last of their clothes and she bent her knees, planting her feet on the mattress. Micah broke the kiss so he could watch her face as their bodies joined. She met his gaze, her hazel eyes shining with joy as they reunited in the most basic, elemental way.

"Micah." His name was a whisper of sound, part benediction, part sigh.

"I'm here," he said, settling into a smooth, easy rhythm. "I'm not going anywhere. I'm never leaving you again."

Chapter 16

The bed was shaking.

Bea came awake with a sudden start, her brain foggy with sleep as she tried to process what was happening. The mattress moved for another second, then stopped. What was going on?

Earthquake?

No. She dismissed the thought almost at once. But what, then?

The movement started up again, and she realized Micah was thrashing next to her. His body jerked and shuddered, causing the whole bed to shake with his movements.

She rolled onto her side, peering at him in the gray light of dawn seeping around the edges of the curtains. He was frowning deeply, his muscles tense as he kicked and rolled, fighting an unseen enemy.

Bea scooted to the edge of the bed and hesitated, not sure of what to do. She'd read somewhere it was dangerous to wake a person when they were in the middle of the nightmare, but he was clearly suffering. Could she really leave him in that hellscape of a dream when she had the power to free him from its clutches?

He let out a pained moan, the sound tearing free from his throat with an effort that broke her heart. Consequences be damned, she wasn't going to let this go on any longer.

Moving carefully, she slipped out of bed and walked around to the other side where he lay, breathing hard. His head rocked back and forth on the pillow, as if he was trying to deny something or erase it from his memory. She considered her options for a beat, trying to figure out the least jarring way to wake him.

In the end, she settled for placing her hand on his lower leg, just under his knee. If he woke up swinging, hopefully she was out of range of his fists.

She shook him gently. "Micah," she said softly.

He moaned but otherwise didn't respond. She tried again, shaking him a little harder this time. "Micah," she said, louder.

Without warning, he jackknifed up on the bed, fists at the ready in a boxer's defensive stance. Bea let go of his leg and scooted back, giving him space. She knew Micah would never intentionally hurt her, but she also knew he'd never forgive himself if he accidentally lashed out and hit her.

His chest heaved as he gasped for air, and his eyes were wide and unfocused. She knew he wasn't really awake yet, so she spoke to him, trying to keep her voice even and calm.

"You're having a nightmare. It's time to wake up now. It's just a dream. It's not real."

He stilled, his body going stiff as she spoke. After a few endless seconds, his shoulders relaxed and he dropped his head.

"Bea?" Her heart ached at the sound of his voice, tired and almost defeated, as if he'd lost some internal battle.

"I'm here." She moved back to the bed and sat, placing her hand on his knee. "You're okay."

"Did I…" He trailed off, and she heard him gulp. "Did I hurt you?"

"No." She took his hand, squeezing for emphasis. "Not at all. I woke up because the bed was moving, and when I realized you were having a nightmare, I couldn't let you go on. It sounded awful."

He sighed and ran a hand through his hair. "They can be pretty intense."

"Do you have them often?"

He shook his head, but the light was too dim for her to see his face clearly. "Not anymore. I mainly get them when I'm stressed about something."

"The case." It wasn't a question—she knew he was upset about finding the bodies in Joey's backyard and the delay in the investigation. He hadn't talked to her about it in detail, but his mood all evening had been proof enough.

He nodded, confirming her suspicions.

"What usually happens when you have a nightmare?"

"Chunk wakes me up. But since he's not here…"

"I think he's still asleep in the kitchen," Bea said. "Maybe he figured I'd take care of you, so he could have the night off."

"He's earned it," Micah replied.

He leaned back against the headboard, and Bea rounded the bed and slipped in beside him again. The sheets were cool, so she snuggled up against his warmth. He put his arm around her, holding her in place.

"Was it about the war?"

He stiffened slightly, and she wondered if she'd made a mistake asking him about the nightmare. But she wanted to know what was bothering him, wanted to help him work through it in any way she could.

He was quiet for so long she began to wonder if he was going to answer her question. When he did finally speak, his voice was no louder than a whisper. "Yes."

"Do you want to talk about it? Maybe if you do, it will help you work through things."

"No." He shook his head, his chin brushing against her hair. "There's no way I'm going to expose you to that. You can't handle it."

Bea bristled at his statement. "I'm tougher than I look," she said, trying to keep her tone light.

Micah ran his hand down her arm. "Some things are too terrible to know. It's better for you to stay in the dark."

She processed his words, trying to see things from his point of view. But all she heard was another man in her life who thought he knew what was best for her.

Frustration welled in her chest, and she suddenly didn't want to touch him anymore. She pushed up, breaking the contact between their bodies. Micah must have sensed the shift in her mood because he turned to face her. "What?"

"You sound like my father."

He reared back as if she'd slapped him. "*What? You can't be serious.*"

"I am. Look, if you don't want to talk about your nightmare because you'd rather not relive it, that's one thing. But if you're holding back because you think I can't handle knowing what you went through during the war, you're treating me like a child."

"I am not—"

"You did the same thing earlier," she continued, cutting off his protest. "You're clearly upset about the case, but you won't talk to me about it, I guess because you think you're protecting me. And while I appreciate the intent, you're not doing me any favors. I'm a grown woman. I want to help you, be a true partner to you, but I can't do that if you keep holding me at arm's length."

He was silent, and after a moment she realized he wasn't going to say anything. "Fenwick thought he knew what was best for me, too. Look how that turned out."

"I'm not your father," he said. There was a note of sadness in his voice she hadn't heard before.

"I know that. But you're treating me the same way he did."

"What are you saying, Bea?"

She sighed, her heart heavy. "I guess I'm asking if you can stop thinking of me as someone you need to protect, and start seeing me as your partner."

"I…" He trailed off, and she blinked as tears stung her eyes. "I don't know." He sounded helpless, as if he wanted to give her a different answer but couldn't.

Bea nodded and slipped out of bed. "Where are you going?" he asked.

"Sun's coming up," she said, gathering her clothes. "Might as well start the day."

"Bea, please don't leave like this—"

"I'm just going to the bathroom." Physically, she wouldn't be going far, but she was already trying to put some emotional distance between them. If Micah couldn't treat her like an equal, they had no future together.

Apparently, he realized the same thing. "Why can't you just trust me? I only want what's best for you."

She shook her head. "This has nothing to do with trust. And I think you know that."

He stared at her from the bed, and in the growing light she could see his expression was one of agonized resignation. The tears began to well in earnest, and for a second, she wanted to run to his side and tell him to forget everything she'd just said. If she put a little effort into it, she could overlook his actions. After all, he was only trying to protect her, right?

It would be a difficult pill to swallow, but if she could accept that there were things Micah was never going to tell her, they could move forward and have a relationship again. She'd have him back in her life, and they could build a future together.

Except…she wanted more than just Micah's physical presence. She wanted all of him—body and soul. And if he was determined to keep parts of his life secret, they'd never have the kind of relationship she wanted.

So, as much as it pained her to do so, Bea had to take a step back. Maybe Micah needed more time to adjust to being around her again. It made sense—they had only just found out about her father's deception. But while she hoped he would come to understand her point of view, she had to prepare for the possibility that he might not change his mind.

"Try to rest," she said, pausing at the door. "We still have a few hours before we need to be anywhere."

He nodded, and as she slipped into the hall, she could have sworn he spoke.

"I'm sorry."

But it was probably just her imagination playing tricks on her.

Later that morning, Micah took a deep breath and walked into the interrogation room. Evan Larson sat at the table, looking bored. His lawyer sat by his side, typing madly on his phone. Probably pulling double duty, working on another case while they waited for the questioning to start. If Evan was bothered by the fact he didn't have his attorney's full attention, he didn't show it. He met Micah's eyes, then glanced at his watch in silent rebuke.

Micah fought to keep a smile off his face. So Larson wasn't happy about the wait. *Good.*

He walked over and sat in the chair opposite Evan, placing the file folder he carried on the table. Inside were printouts of the photos he'd taken of Evan and Thad in the park and crime scene photos of Thad's body being recovered from the shallow grave in Joey's backyard. But Micah didn't reach for them yet. He wanted to talk to Larson, get a feel for his mood before he went in for the kill.

"Glad you could join us this morning," Micah said.

Evan arched one brow. "You guys didn't give me much of a choice."

"This investigation is a priority," Micah replied. "I'm sure you can appreciate that."

"Which investigation?" asked the attorney, slipping his phone into his jacket pocket. "I'm sure the department has several ongoing cases. The officers weren't clear as to which one was relevant to Mr. Larson."

Micah ignored the man, instead focusing on Evan. "How do you know Joey McBurn?"

Larson's bored expression remained, but he began to tap his index finger on the table. Micah noticed the gesture but didn't call attention to it.

So, you do know Joey, he thought, feeling a spurt of triumph. He hadn't expected it to be this easy—the Teflon Twins were usually more careful about giving away information.

"I don't think I know anyone by that name," Evan said. "But it sounds familiar. Where have I heard it before?"

"He's the latest victim of the Groom Killer," his attorney said. The man turned to look at Micah. "Is that why we're here? You really suspect my client of being the Groom Killer?" His tone was incredulous, as if he couldn't believe Micah or anyone else would entertain such a crazy idea.

"I didn't say that," Micah replied evenly. "Right now, I'm just asking questions."

"Officer, if you've brought Mr. Larson in for a fishing expedition, I can tell you it's a waste of time. And I will personally see to it that you are reprimanded for your actions."

Micah ignored the man's posturing and focused on Evan. "So, you don't know Joey? Or should I say, you didn't know Joey?"

Larson shrugged one shoulder. "That's what I said."

"What about his fiancée?"

"What about her?"

"It's my understanding you had a relationship with her before she started dating Joey McBurn. Would you care to comment on that?"

Larson picked an invisible piece of lint off the cuff of his suit jacket. He was trying to appear calm and collected, but Micah saw the lines of strain around his eyes and knew he was worried. "What's her name? I date a lot of women."

"Angelina Cooper."

Evan nodded slowly. "I think I remember her. She's a waitress, right?"

Micah nodded. "She says that's how you met."

Larson leaned forward. "Yeah, it's coming back to me now. We went out a few times. Had a little fun. But it didn't go anywhere."

"So you haven't been in contact with her since the two of you stopped seeing each other?"

"Nope. I moved on to the next willing woman. I don't stay lonely for long." His grin was more of a leer that made Micah's stomach turn.

Excitement thrummed in Micah's veins as he opened the file folder. He retrieved a piece of paper and slid it across the table so Evan and his attorney could look at it. "Can you please explain why your phone number turned up in Ms. Cooper's phone records over the last three weeks? I've marked each call in yellow to make it easier for you to see."

Evan said nothing, but his eyes flared and a muscle in his jaw tensed. He glanced at his attorney, who shook his head.

"I'm just wondering why you said you haven't had any contact with her when the records clearly show you have called her at least five times in the recent past."

"This proves nothing," Larson's attorney said. He pushed the paper away with an expression of contempt. "All this shows is that my client's phone was used to dial Ms. Cooper. You have no way to determine who actually made the call. It's possible someone else was using Mr. Larson's phone without his knowledge. Furthermore, none of the calls last longer than ten seconds, suggesting no conversation actually took place."

Micah smiled indulgently. It was a bogus excuse, and they all knew it. Still, at least the man was earning his money today.

"What's the nature of your relationship with Thad Randall?"

Evan leaned back, a glint of anger in his eyes. "I have no relationship with him."

Micah nodded, pretending to accept that response. "I see." He opened the file folder again, this time withdrawing the photos he'd taken of the two men in the park. "These were taken two days ago. Is that you?"

Larson didn't even bother to look at the pictures. "Could be. Might also be my brother."

"That's possible," Micah said. "Which is why we're also questioning him right now, as well."

Fear flashed in Evan's gaze, there and gone in a second. But it was enough to tell Micah he was on the right track. Either Larson was worried he was going to go down for Thad's murder, or he was scared of his brother's response to being questioned. Which meant they both had something to hide.

"See, I'm thinking this is you," Micah said, stabbing at the picture with his finger. "And I'm wondering what you and Thad were talking about. You both seem so serious."

Larson didn't reply, but his attorney spoke. "You haven't established this is my client. Move on, please."

Once again, Micah ignored the man. This was his show, and he wasn't going to let some slick lawyer determine the course of his interrogation.

He kept quiet, watching Larson. He knew from experience that most people weren't comfortable with silence, and would often start talking simply to fill the space. Many criminals had inadvertently implicated themselves or even confessed in their rush to speak. Maybe Micah would be so lucky today.

Evan shifted in his chair, his cool facade cracking a bit. He kept glancing at his attorney, and Micah got the impression that if the lawyer hadn't been present, Larson would have had a lot to say.

Micah let him squirm a bit longer, enjoying the moment. Finally, Larson spoke. "We were in high school together. I just ran into him… I mean, if that's even me in the photo."

And there it is, Micah thought, satisfaction blooming in his chest.

"Mr. Larson, I think you should stop talking." His attorney's tone was urgent, but the damage had already been done.

"Just two old friends, was that it?"

Evan started to nod, but stopped when his lawyer touched his arm.

"Since you two were so close, I imagine it will upset you to learn Thad Randall was found dead yesterday afternoon." Micah opened the folder again, this time withdrawing the photos from the backyard exhumation. He slid them across the table, keeping his eyes glued to Evan's face.

He detected another flash of fear as Larson sucked in a breath. Micah gave Evan a moment to study the pictures, then leaned forward. "Now it's time for you to tell me where you were and what you were doing yesterday morning."

"You think I did this?" Larson tried to sound outraged, but he wasn't convincing anyone.

Micah leaned back and shrugged. "Try to see it from my perspective. Two days ago, I saw you and Thad deep in conversation. Then yesterday I found Thad's body buried in Joey McBurn's backyard. The same Joey McBurn who was engaged to Angelina Cooper, a woman you used to date and are still calling, if the phone records are to be believed."

Evan's forehead glistened with a fine sheen of sweat. He thrust his hand into his jacket and withdrew a long leather wallet, which he unfolded. After a few seconds, he removed a slip of paper and tossed it on the table.

"The receipt from breakfast yesterday," he said, sounding a little smug.

"Was it just you?" Micah asked. "How do I know it wasn't your brother pretending to be you?"

Larson's smile was triumphant. "We were both there."

Damn. So much for that theory. Still, it didn't mean Larson was in the clear. The medical examiner hadn't finished examining the bodies yet—it was entirely possible Thad Randall had been killed the day before yesterday, which meant Evan's alibi didn't apply. And he wouldn't put it past the man to hire out his dirty work...

"This is all very interesting," said Larson's attorney. "But I'm not seeing anything here that goes beyond coincidence." He pushed back from the table, and after a second, Evan did the same.

Micah stood, as well, his frustration mounting. Unfortunately, Larson's lawyer was right. Everything he had right now was circumstantial, at best. He'd been hoping Evan would incriminate himself, but his attorney had prevented that from happening.

"I assume we're done here?" the lawyer asked.

"For now," Micah said. He leaned forward to gather the phone records and photographs, tapping them neatly back into the file folder. "Don't leave town, Evan. I might need to speak to you again."

"Whatever you say, officer." Larson's tone was all sweetness and light, as if he was just another law-abiding citizen who was happy to assist in any way possible.

Micah watched the two men leave, anger building in his chest. It felt like this investigation was slipping through his fingers, and he had a sinking suspicion that the Teflon Twins were going to get away with murder.

He stepped into the hall to find Brayden standing there, watching Larson and his lawyer leave. "Any luck?"

Micah shook his head. "Not really. It's obvious Evan knows something, but his attorney is too smart to let him put his foot in it. You?"

Brayden sighed. "Same. Except Noel has enough self-control to conceal his reactions. I think they're definitely involved in the murders of the two guys you found yesterday, but unless they slip up, I don't know that we'll be able to pin it on them."

"Figures." Would they ever catch a break?

He and Brayden set off for the main squad room, each man lost in his own thoughts. Micah noticed the message light on his desk phone was blinking, and he punched in the number to find the lab had news for him. After a quick call, he walked over to Brayden's desk to give him the update.

"Evidence analysis on Tucker Frane is back," he said, referring to the dead witness who claimed to have seen Demi shoot Joey McBurn.

"And?"

"No gunshot residue on his hands."

"Damn," Brayden muttered. "I knew it was a long shot to think he might be Joey's killer, but I was still hopeful."

"I know what you mean," Micah said. "It would have been nice to close at least one case."

Brayden cocked his head to the side, studying Micah. "You doing okay?"

Micah felt his shoulders stiffen involuntarily. "Yeah. Why?"

Brayden shrugged. "You seem a little…off this morning."

Lack of sleep will do that to a man, Micah thought sarcastically. Last night had gone so well. Until it hadn't, and Bea had left him sitting in the bed alone as dawn came creeping through the curtains.

You're treating me like a child.

Her words echoed in his head, a relentless drumbeat he couldn't escape.

His first instinct had been to deny it. Couldn't she see he was trying to protect her from the ugliness in his world? That he didn't want to expose her to all the darkness for no good reason?

It was difficult for him to understand why she was so upset, why she'd decided to ruin a perfectly nice evening with an argument. He'd spent hours trying to see things from her perspective, but he hadn't been able to make the leap.

He'd hoped having Bea back in his life would help him deal with the stress of his job and his past, but that certainly wasn't the case right now. Knowing that she was unhappy with him made his heart sink, but for the life of him, he didn't know what to do to fix things. It was his nature to want to protect her, and he couldn't simply ignore his instincts in order to appease her feelings.

"Yeah." Micah sighed heavily, feeling the weight of the world on his shoulders. He glanced around to make sure they were alone. Bea was in the break room with Chunk, and the rest of the department was busy at their own desks. For all intents and purposes, he and Brayden were alone.

"It's Bea," he said, careful to keep his voice low.

"You guys back together?"

"I thought so. Now I'm not so sure. We had an argument last night."

Brayden leaned back and put his feet on his desk. "You guys have been apart for a while. Maybe it's just getting-to-know-you pains."

Micah shook his head. "I don't think so. She accused me of keeping things from her. Said I was treating her like a child because I don't share everything with her."

"Is she right?"

Micah pulled over a chair and sat. "Maybe. I don't tell her all the details of work or my time in the army, but that's because I don't want her to hear about those terrible things. I'm sure she could handle it, but why should I expose her to that?"

Brayden nodded. "I hear you. I'd probably do the same thing if I was in a relationship."

Micah threw his hands in the air. "Thank you. I've been stewing over this all morning, wondering if I was being unreasonable."

"I don't think you are," Brayden said. "But, keep in mind, I haven't had a ton of luck with women."

Micah heard a snort behind him and turned to find Finn standing nearby. "Something you wanna add, chief?"

Finn chuckled softly. "I don't think you want to hear my opinion."

"No, come on. Lay it on me. You're in a happy relationship. What's your secret?"

Finn perched on the edge of Brayden's desk and crossed his arms. "You really want to know? It's not easy."

"Chief, do you know what they do to you in Ranger school? I think I can handle it."

Finn's smile took on a condescending edge. "Communication."

"Communication?" echoed Brayden.

"Yep. That's the secret. You have to talk to each other."

Micah frowned. "You're saying you tell Darby everything about your day? Even the dark, unsavory parts?"

Finn shrugged. "I don't give her a detailed play-by-play, but I tell her the gist of things, yeah. If I didn't talk to her, I'd probably go mad."

Micah was silent, considering the man's words. Finally, he spoke. "I don't know if I can do that." He ran a hand through his hair, trying to figure out the best way to verbalize his thoughts. "I've spent so long keeping everything to myself. I'm not sure I can talk about things I'd really rather forget. Why put those memories in her head, when I hate having them in my own?"

"I can't answer that," Finn said, clapping him on the back. "But I know talking to Darby works for me. Maybe you and Bea will have to figure out another arrangement."

The chief's advice made sense, but Micah didn't

think Bea would accept anything less than full and open communication.

Unfortunately, he wasn't sure that was something he could give her.

Chapter 17

Bea flipped the Closed sign over, displaying to one and all that the boutique was once again ready for business. Micah had asked if they could come to her store later in the day so that he could take the morning to interview Evan Larson. Figuring she didn't have a long line of brides waiting for the shop to open, she'd agreed.

Micah had been nothing but pleasant to her this morning after she'd emerged from the guest bedroom. It was as if their earlier conversation hadn't happened. But even though he was pretending everything was fine, she sensed a wall between them. She felt a separation now that hadn't been there before. She had hoped that telling him her worries and her needs would help their relationship grow stronger, but instead they'd taken a step back.

Maybe several steps back.

She sighed quietly, glancing over at him with a subtle turn of her head. He was standing by the register counter, Chunk sitting patiently at his feet. She wanted to give him time to process what they had talked about, but she also wanted to know what he was thinking. If Micah couldn't open up and really share with her, they didn't have a future. And that was something she needed to know sooner rather than later. The more time they spent together, the longer they were around each other, the harder it would be for her to walk away.

She walked over to the counter, straightening dresses as she moved through the store. Micah pocketed his cell phone as she approached. "Mind if I step out for a few minutes? I figured I'd take Chunk to the park for a potty break, then grab us a couple of coffees on the way back. I'll keep my eye on the store the whole time, but since it's been quiet the last few days, I think you'll be fine."

"That sounds nice." Bea said. She offered him a polite smile, playing along with the fiction that everything was fine between them. "I need to call a few more vendors, anyway." She'd spent the morning in the squad's break room while he interviewed Larson, chatting with suppliers about long-standing orders. Given the precarious state of her finances, she was having to make some tough calls about inventory and other accessories. She hated scaling back on the diversity of products she was able to offer to brides, but at the same time, she couldn't go bankrupt stocking the boutique with items no one was buying.

The tension drained from her muscles as soon as Micah left the store. She shouldn't feel so anxious around the man she loved, damn it! But until they straightened things out between them, she was going to be walking on eggshells.

She'd just finished her first call when the bell over the door tinkled, announcing the arrival of a customer. Bea looked up to find Angelina Cooper, Joey's fiancée, standing just inside the doorway. She looked a little lost, as if she didn't quite know what she was doing.

Bea's heart went out to the woman. It was clear her grief was taking a toll on her body; her face was lined, her hair limp and her shoulders slumped. But her eyes burned bright with an emotion Bea couldn't quite place. Anger? Determination? Or something else?

"Angelina." Bea walked over to the woman, her hand extended. "I'm so sorry for your loss. What can I do for you?"

Angelina met her gaze and reared back a little, as if surprised to see Bea in the store. "Oh!" She shook her head and cleared her throat. "I was just… I was in the neighborhood, and thought…" She blinked back tears and tried again. "I just wanted to see the room. Where he died. It was the last place he was alive, and I need to see it."

Bea frowned. That didn't sound like such a good idea to her, but what did she know about it? If seeing the fitting room would somehow help Angelina process her grief over losing Joey, then who was Bea to stop her?

"Can I go back?"

Bea nodded. "Sure. I'll give you some time."

"Thank you." Angelina sniffed and walked past, and as she moved, Bea caught a whiff of her perfume.

I know that scent...

All at once, Bea was thrust back to that night when she was closing up alone and the power had been switched off. She heard again the rustling in the store, her skin prickling anew with the remembered sense of someone coming closer in the darkness. Then a breath of perfume followed by blinding pain.

She put her hand to her head and took a step back, instinctively trying to protect herself from the anticipated blow. But it never came.

Angelina stared at her, recognition dawning on her face. "You know, don't you?"

"It was you." Bea didn't bother asking—she was certain. "You hit me that night."

Angelina bit her lip and nodded, fresh tears welling in her eyes. "I did. I never meant to hurt you."

"Why were you here?" Bea's stomach sank as she answered her own question. "Oh, my God—you killed Joey."

"No!" Angelina practically screamed the word, her voice hoarse with emotion. "No, I would never do that. I came here for the dress. The one I wanted but couldn't afford. I was going to steal it."

Bea gaped at her, dumbfounded. "Did you think I

wouldn't recognize the dress as one of my own when you walked down the aisle?"

Angelina shook her head. "I wasn't thinking that far ahead. I made it as far as the stockroom, and then the lights went out. I got spooked, so I tried to run. But then you walked in front of me, so I panicked." She began to pace a few steps, back and forth, her hands clutching her hair as she walked.

Come on, Micah, where are you? Bea knew she needed to keep Angelina in the store so Micah could arrest her, but the woman was becoming increasingly emotional and Bea wasn't sure how much longer she'd stick around.

"It's fine," Bea said, trying to calm her down. "It was just a misunderstanding. No hard feelings."

Angelina stopped pacing and turned to look at her. There was a deep sadness in her eyes that sent a chill skittering down Bea's spine. Angelina looked like a woman who had decided to do a bad thing, and Bea had a sick feeling she wasn't going to like whatever happened next.

"No, it's not fine. It will never be fine again." Angelina dipped her hand into her purse and withdrew a small black gun. She pointed it directly at Bea, and Bea felt her heart stall in her chest. Angelina let out a sob. "I had no idea that while I was trying to steal my wedding gown, Joey was dying in the fitting room." Another wail escaped her.

"Angelina, you don't have to do this." Bea took a step back, her hands up by her ears. "I'm not going to press charges. There's no need for violence."

"Don't you see?" the woman whispered. Tears streamed down her face and the gun wobbled as her hand shook. "I have nothing left to live for. Joey is dead. The man I love is gone, and nothing will ever bring him back."

Her despair was palpable, a mirror of Bea's own emotions in the weeks after she'd received the forged breakup letter. For a split second, Bea saw herself in Angelina. She could have easily fallen into the same kind of emotional black hole and decided to give up.

But she was a fighter. She hadn't surrendered then, and she wasn't about to start now.

Bea planted her feet, knowing that retreat was useless. "Angelina," she said firmly. "Put the gun down. You don't want to shoot me, and I don't want anyone to get hurt."

The woman blinked at her, clearly surprised by the order. Her hand wavered, the gun lowering by a few inches.

"That's good," Bea said encouragingly. "Just put it on the floor."

Angelina dropped her arm, nodding blankly. But just as Bea thought it was safe to take a breath, Angelina pointed the gun at her again. "No," she said, shaking her head. "I lost everything. You have no idea what that's like, how much pain I'm in."

Bea said nothing. Now was not the time to try to explain her own past heartbreak. Angelina wasn't stable enough to listen, and Bea didn't want to get shot for saying the wrong thing.

"I'm sorry," Angelina said. She swiped at her eyes and sniffed again. "It wasn't supposed to be like this."

"Nothing's happened yet," Bea said, trying to keep her voice calm. "You can still walk out of here."

"No." Angelina smiled sadly. "I can't."

Bea watched in horror as Angelina pointed the gun at her own head. Without thinking, she lunged forward, grabbing Angelina's arm. The woman shrieked and the gun went off with a thunderous boom that made Bea's ears ring.

Fiery pain stabbed Bea's side as they landed on the floor in a heap. She tried to move, but her muscles refused to cooperate. Angelina squirmed out from underneath her, rudely kicking and pushing in a bid for freedom. Bea tried to grab the woman's ankle, but it was no use. Her movements were uncoordinated and slow, making her feel like she was swimming through a vat of molasses.

"Stop," she tried to say. As if the word would magically hold Angelina there until Micah returned. Bea closed her eyes as the floor trembled with the pressure of footsteps. Angelina was getting away.

The air around her moved, and Bea realized with a start she was *feeling* the vibrations of a dog's bark. She turned her head to find Chunk snarling at Angelina, his four paws firmly planted and his stout body braced for a fight. Micah was standing behind the woman, snapping cuffs around her wrists. But his eyes were on Bea, his face pale as he stared down at her.

As soon as Angelina had been restrained, Micah

dropped to his knees. His lips moved, but Bea couldn't understand he was saying. Her ears were still ringing from the gunshot, and a spike of panic hit her as she wondered if she'd ever be able to hear again.

Micah zeroed in on her side and he lifted up her shirt to press his big hand against her skin. He bore down, the pressure triggering a fresh wave of pain that made her see stars. In his other hand he punched numbers into his phone.

"We have to stop meeting like this," she mumbled. Or, at least, that's what she tried to say. Micah's green gaze darted back to her face, his expression incredulous. He leaned down, and she faintly heard his voice near her ear.

"Stick with the boutique. Comedy's not your thing."

She opened her mouth to reply, but he pressed harder on her wound and her words came out as a groan. His eyes were full of apology, and he mouthed the word, "Sorry."

"It's okay," she said. She shivered, feeling suddenly cold. Black spots danced in her vision, and as she looked at Micah, he seemed to recede into the far distance.

His face changed before her eyes, his expression morphing from concern to panic. His mouth opened, his touch growing rough as his free hand grabbed her shoulder hard.

She thought she heard him yell, "Stay with me!" But the black spots grew and coalesced until they obscured her vision, and she sank into darkness.

* * *

Micah sat next to Bea's hospital bed, his eyes glued to her face as he watched for any signs of trouble, any tightening of muscle or subtle grimace that might indicate she was in pain. She seemed calm, if a bit groggy from the medication they'd given her once they'd reached the hospital.

The residual adrenaline in his system made him twitchy, and he bounced his leg up and down in a bid to expel his nervous energy. Even though the doctor had assured him Bea would make a full recovery, he still couldn't get over the sight of her on the floor of the boutique, bloody and helpless.

"The bullet missed all the important parts," the doctor had said. "She's very lucky. I stitched her up and we'll give her some fluids. She should be free to go in a few hours."

Micah had nodded mechanically, hearing the woman's words but not really absorbing them. It was only when he'd seen Bea in the hospital bed that he'd begun to relax, able to convince himself that she was okay.

She opened her eyes and frowned slightly when she saw him. "You're still here. I thought I told you go to home and rest."

"You did," he said, leaning forward to take her hand. "But I'm not going anywhere until you do."

"What about Chunk?"

"He's with Brayden." Backup had arrived quickly. Brayden had taken one look at the scene and told

Micah to stay with Bea. He'd promised to take care of Chunk, and Micah knew he could trust his friend.

"He was really something today," Bea said, a note of wonder in her voice. "I didn't think he had it in him to be vicious, but he looked like he wanted to take a bite out of Angelina."

"Everyone's got a line," Micah said. A spike of guilt pierced his chest as he remembered Chunk's initial reaction to Angelina when he'd gone to her apartment to question her. *He was trying to tell me then.* But Micah had been too shortsighted to realize it, and now Bea was paying the price.

A knock sounded on the door, and they both turned to see Fenwick poke his head into the room. "May I?" He sounded uncharacteristically quiet, and Micah had to wonder if his argument with Bea had upset him more than he'd shown her.

Micah glanced back at Bea, gauging her reaction. Her jaw set and she lifted one brow in a subtle challenge, but she nodded.

Fenwick entered the room and closed the door behind him. For a moment, he simply stood in place, his eyes searching Bea's face as if to reassure himself she was fine. Then he spoke. "Are you okay?"

She nodded. "Yes. Thanks to Micah."

Her father turned to look at him for the first time. He nodded once in acknowledgment, or perhaps thanks. "May I have a moment with my daughter please?" His tone was polite, but there was a thin edge of ice Micah picked up on right away.

"No." They both turned to Bea, who grabbed

Micah's hand, anchoring him in place. "Anything you have to say to me you will say in front of Micah."

Fenwick's mouth tightened, but he didn't press the issue. Micah remained still, trying to be as unobtrusive as possible. He was happy to support Bea, but he didn't want to aggravate her father and make the situation more difficult for her.

Fenwick glanced down, then took a deep breath and faced Micah. "I suppose thanks are in order," he said quietly. "This is the second time you've saved my daughter from danger."

"You never have to thank me for that."

Fenwick nodded, his gaze assessing. "It seems I may have underestimated you, young man. I'm sorry for that."

Micah blinked, hardly daring to believe his ears. Had Bea's father actually apologized to him?

Fenwick turned back to Bea. "I've been thinking a lot about our conversation. I don't want to lose you, Beatrix. I know you don't think I care about you, but that simply isn't true. You're my daughter, and I love you."

"You have a funny way of showing it."

Fenwick looked down, his cheeks flushing. Micah could tell this was hard on the man, but he felt no sympathy for his struggles. Instead, he was worried about Bea and how she was feeling in the wake of the shooting. The last thing she needed was for this encounter to turn into another argument—that wouldn't be good for her recovery.

The older man lifted his head and looked at Bea.

"I made a mistake," he said. Micah could tell by the tone of Fenwick's voice that he was having a difficult time admitting he had been wrong. Apologies did not come naturally to the man, and it seemed he was quite out of practice.

Bea said nothing. She simply stared at her father, her silence louder than any words.

Fenwick sighed, clearly growing impatient. He had probably figured he'd waltz in, offer a weak apology and bask in the glow of Bea's immediate forgiveness. Micah almost shook his head at the thought. The man obviously didn't know a thing about his headstrong daughter if he imagined she'd cave that easily.

"I'm sorry, Bea. Is that what you want to hear?"

"Yes." Her voice was quiet, her tone almost lethal. "I deserve an apology. We both do."

Fenwick straightened his spine, and Micah figured the man was about to unleash a verbal tirade. *Here we go…*

He opened his mouth, then seemed to suddenly deflate. "I know," he said. "And I'm sorry." He turned to look at Micah. "I wronged you both."

Bea's grip on his hand tightened, and Micah realized she was shocked by her father's words.

"This isn't easy for me," Fenwick continued. "I thought I was doing the right thing. But I realize now I was wrong. And I'm sorry for the pain that caused you."

"Thank you," Bea said.

"Will you forgive me?" Fenwick looked at Micah with an appealing expression.

Micah shook his head. "I'm not the one you need to convince."

They both turned to Bea, who watched her father carefully. "I can't snap my fingers and forget what you did," she said finally. "But if you're truly sorry, then I accept your apology. And I will try to move past your actions."

Fenwick's breath rushed out, and Micah realized just how nervous the older man had been. He'd covered his nerves with bluster and posturing, but it seemed he really had been worried about Bea's reaction.

"Thank you," he said. He approached the bed and leaned in to kiss Bea's cheek. She stiffened, and he apparently thought better of the gesture. Instead, he reached for her free hand and gave it a squeeze. "I'll leave you to rest now. Let me know if you need anything."

He turned and offered Micah a nod, then headed for the door. As soon as he'd left, Bea let out a heavy sigh.

"Well. That was…interesting."

"I think his apology was genuine," Micah said.

She arched one eyebrow, her expression skeptical. "Perhaps. Time will tell, I suppose." She let go of his hand, and Micah realized he was being dismissed.

Sure enough, her next words proved his suspicion correct. "You probably have work to do. Why don't you head in to the station?"

A flutter of panic made his stomach turn. Was she telling him to leave because she no longer wanted him around? Did she really think he'd prioritize his work over her? He remembered their earlier conversation, the way she'd compared him to her father. Had seeing the man reminded her of the same?

Micah didn't know what to say, but he could feel a gulf forming between them. If he didn't start building a bridge now, he might never be able to reach her again.

"You're more important to me than my job," he said. "I'm not going to leave you to sit in this hospital room alone. Not unless that's what you really want." He wasn't going to force his presence on her, but he wasn't going to simply walk away, either. If Bea truly wanted him to leave, she was going to have to spell it out in no uncertain terms.

She was quiet a moment, feeding his fear that she truly wanted him gone. If she turned him away now, would he ever be able to win her back?

Finally, she shook her head. "All right," she said quietly. "You can stay. But I don't want to talk right now."

"We don't have to." He'd never been good at talking, anyway, which was part of their current problem.

He turned his hand palm up on her bed in silent invitation. After what seemed like an eternity, she slipped her hand into his, and they sat in silence, each lost in their own thoughts.

Micah knew he couldn't fix things today, and he wasn't sure how long Bea's patience would last. But they had this moment, and for now, it was enough.

Chapter 18

The next few days passed with agonizing slowness. Bea had been released from the hospital with strict instructions to rest.

"No going back to work for at least a week," the doctor had said.

Bea had tried to protest. "But my job isn't strenuous!"

The woman had merely tilted her head down to stare at Bea over the rims of her glasses. "I'll say it again, in case I wasn't clear the first time. No working for at least a week."

"What am I supposed to do, exactly?"

"Rest. Take naps. Watch TV. Read trashy novels. In short, take a vacation from life."

Micah had stepped in. "I'll make sure she takes it easy, doc."

He'd offered to let Bea continue to stay with him, but she had turned him down. She wanted to be in her own space again, to be surrounded by her own things and to feel at home. Besides, she'd figured the separation would do them both some good.

She'd resigned herself to a week of boredom, but over the past few days she'd had a steady stream of visitors. One of her sisters stopped by every morning, and she'd enjoyed catching up with them and hearing about what was going on in their lives. Patience told her all about the puppies' training progress, while Gemma talked about her latest shopping adventures. Even Layla had taken time away from her job as VP of Colton Energy to stop by and chat for a couple of hours. In a way, the time with her sisters had been a silver lining to this whole mess.

To her surprise, Micah had stopped by every afternoon with Chunk. The pair had gotten into the habit of coming over just after lunch and they stayed until the last of the dinner dishes was put away. She'd asked him about his work, but Micah told her that Finn was giving him a bit of a break so he could make sure her recovery went well. At first, Bea had thought being around Micah would feel awkward in light of their unspoken issues, but they'd soon fallen into an easy rhythm and she'd come to look forward to his visits.

Maybe she should just let it go and accept that Micah wasn't going to share every aspect of his life with her. They were compatible in so many other ways—did it really matter that he kept part of himself back?

"He's allowed to have his own secrets," she muttered.

But it wasn't really about secrets, she knew. If he didn't want to share something with her, that was one thing. But if he deliberately withheld things from her because he figured she couldn't handle them, that was quite another. Open communication was required for their relationship to work. If anything, the forged letters had taught her that. If either one of them had been able to reach the other after receiving the letter, they wouldn't have been apart for ten years.

Maybe they'd moved too fast, she mused. They'd jumped headlong into this relationship, driven by a sense of urgency to make up for lost time. But had that been the right choice? If they had taken more time to get to know each other again, would they be having this issue now?

Her thoughts were interrupted by the chime of the doorbell. She opened the door to find Micah on the stoop, Chunk at his feet. The dog's tail began to thump against the floor as soon as he saw her, and Bea swore he was grinning, at least as much as his saggy jowls would allow.

She smiled, unable to remain pensive while Chunk was around. She'd never considered herself a dog person before, but there was something about Chunk that gave her the warm fuzzies.

"Come in," she said, taking a step back. Man and dog both entered her apartment. Micah veered off into the kitchen to deposit the grocery bag he was carrying, while Chunk headed for the living room and her couch.

"How are you feeling today?" Micah called out. She heard the sack rustle and figured he was unpacking food. He'd proved himself to be an adequate cook over the last few days, and while Bea felt a little strange about being waited on hand and foot, she wasn't quite up to cooking for herself just yet.

"Not bad," she said. She locked the door and headed for the kitchen.

"Any pain?"

She paused in the doorway and shrugged, then immediately wished she hadn't as the movement tugged on her stitches. "Only if I move wrong."

"Are you staying on top of your medication?"

"Yes, Nurse Nightingale," she said sweetly.

Micah eyed her suspiciously. "I hope you're telling the truth. Otherwise, I'm liable to turn into Nurse Ratched."

She laughed, then gripped her side with a grimace.

"That's it." Micah set down the can he was holding and moved toward her. "Off your feet." He led her into the living room and hovered over her while she sat on the couch. Chunk gave her a friendly swipe with his tongue and settled in beside her for his afternoon nap.

Micah brought the ottoman over and lifted her feet. "Here you go," he said, propping them up on the padded surface. "Now, stay put and I'll get you something to drink. Have you had lunch yet?"

"No," Bea said, knowing it was pointless to resist. Truth be told, a small part of her enjoyed the fuss. It was nice to be the sole focus of Micah's attention, even though it was only temporary.

Actions speak louder than words, her heart said. And no matter how worried Bea was over their block in communication, it was clear Micah cared for her very much.

He returned a few minutes later with a glass of ice water and sandwiches. "I took the liberty of making one for myself. I didn't get a chance to eat yet, either."

"Busy morning?"

He nodded and sat in the chair next to her. "Oh, yeah. We closed your case, but we're no closer to finding the Groom Killer."

"I take it Angelina didn't see anything that night?"

Micah shook his head as he chewed. "Nope. And we know from the forensic evidence our killer is right-handed. Since she's left-handed, that clears her as a suspect."

Bea frowned. "Did you really think she killed Joey? She was so distraught—she was ready to commit suicide over his death."

"True, but that didn't necessarily make her innocent. It was possible she killed him and then felt bad about it."

"I suppose." She took a bite of her sandwich. "I guess it's a good thing I'm not a cop. I'm not suspicious enough for the job."

Micah chuckled. "You learn real quick not to take people at face value."

"Does that bother you?"

He took a deep breath, and for a second Bea expected him to clam up. It was exactly the type of question he normally shied away from answering, and she wanted to kick herself for asking it.

But to her surprise, Micah nodded. "Yeah, sometimes it does. I don't like cynicism, and there are times I have to actively fight against becoming too jaded. I don't want to burn out, or become the lonely old guy who never found love because he was too afraid to connect with people."

A candle of hope lit in her chest and she hardly dared to breathe for fear he would stop talking.

Micah met her gaze, his green eyes bright and earnest. "I've thought a lot about what you said the other day. About how I'm patronizing you by not sharing parts of my life. And I want you to know that's not my intention. I want us to be together—hell, I need you now more than ever."

"I need you, too," she said quietly.

Micah nodded. "I'm glad to hear that." He paused, as if weighing his words. "After the letters, I never really had a long-term relationship with a woman. I dated some, but things were always casual. No one ever wanted to hear my thoughts or really connect with me the way you do. And the guys in my unit, we didn't do the whole touchy-feely thing. I spoke to my therapist, but it was his job to listen to me."

"What are you saying?"

He sighed. "I'm saying I'm not used to having someone in my life who expects me to share the way you do. That's not a bad thing—I know communication is important in a relationship. It's something I'm going to work on, but I need to know if you're willing to give me time to figure this out."

"Yes." She said the word before he'd even finished speaking. "Yes, Micah. I will. We will work on it together."

"You mean that?" She heard the note of hope in his voice, an echo of her own.

"I do. I don't expect you to be perfect."

"That's good, because I know I'm going to make mistakes."

Bea pushed herself up and stepped over to him.

"Whoa," he said, reaching out to steady her. She dropped into his lap, needing to touch him.

"We're both going to make mistakes," she said, stroking the side of his face with her fingertips. "And we'll work through them together."

He pressed his forehead to hers and wrapped his arms around her. "You don't know how happy I am to hear you say that."

She smiled and kissed him softly. "Oh, I think I have an idea."

He sighed and she melted against him. "Seeing you on the floor took years off my life," he said softly. "I can't lose you, Bea. Not again."

Her heart was so full she thought it might burst in her chest. "I'm not going anywhere, Micah," she said. "Not without you."

He kissed her then, tenderly, almost reverently. Tears stung her eyes as she kissed him back, trying to pour all her love into the gesture. After a moment, she pulled back.

"Stay with me tonight?"

Micah's eyes widened. "I don't think that's what the doctor had in mind when she told you to rest."

Bea smiled. "Then just hold me. I don't want you to leave."

Understanding shone in his eyes. "Then I won't. But I should warn you. Chunk snores."

The dog in question let out a sleepy snort, and they both laughed.

"I'll let you in on a little secret," she said, leaning in for another kiss.

"Oh? What's that?"

She nibbled on his bottom lip and spoke the words against his mouth.

"You do, too."

"Any other updates?" Finn glanced around the room, waiting to see if anyone would respond. When no one did, he nodded. "Okay. I have one more thing and then we're done." He glanced at the paper in his hand. "We have a request from a filmmaker who is working on a documentary piece about the Groom Killer. Her name is Esmee da Costa, and she's been bugging me nonstop to tag along with one of the officers working the case."

A low grumble erupted from the assembled group, and Finn held up his hand. "I know, I know. I told her it was too dangerous, not to mention counterproductive to my team. But the woman's relentless. She said she'd settle for interviewing one of you.

Wants to talk to someone related to Demi Colton, since she's hoping to get a personal take on things."

Everyone's head swiveled to focus on Brayden. Micah watched as the tips of his friend's ears turned red.

"No," he said, shaking his head firmly. "No way."

"I don't blame you," Finn said. "And I'm not going to throw you under the bus and insist you talk to her. But be aware she's quite persistent, and she might come looking for you on her own."

"She can look all she wants," Brayden said. "Doesn't mean I'm going to talk to her."

"Fair enough," Finn replied. "Like I said, I can't force you to do anything." With that, the team meeting was over and everyone dispersed to their desks. Micah walked over to Brayden.

"You okay?"

Brayden shook his head. "Fine. I just can't believe the nerve of some people."

"You know the drill. Sex and murder sell. This is getting to be a famous case. Stands to reason people are going to want to find a way to cash in on it."

"Maybe so," Brayden replied. "But I'd never sell out my sister for the sake of a buck."

"I know that." Micah clapped his friend on the back. "Just stay strong. If you ignore her long enough, she might go away."

"You really think I'll get that lucky?"

Micah laughed. "You can hope."

Brayden eyed him suspiciously. "You're in an awfully good mood today."

"Am I?"

"Don't play coy. You can't pull it off. I take it things are going well with Bea?"

Micah couldn't stop a smile from spreading across his face. "Yeah. Really well."

Thanks to Bea's injury, they couldn't do much physically. So they'd spent the last week talking, reconnecting with each other both intellectually and emotionally. He'd started to tell her about his time in the war, and she hadn't flinched when he'd shared some of the tougher stuff he'd dealt with in the desert. She'd told him all about the business, her fears and worries, and what she hoped to accomplish in the future.

He was surprised by how good it felt to open up to Bea, to share with her some of the things he'd rather forget. Micah had expected telling her about his darker moments would cause him to relive them, but that wasn't the case. He felt lighter after their talks, almost as if the act of speaking had robbed the memories of some of their power.

It wasn't just the talking that eased him, though. He knew from his therapy sessions that telling someone about his experiences helped, but it was the fact that he was talking to Bea that made all the difference. She was his safe place, his haven. His home. And today, he was going to show her just how much she meant to him.

"I'm happy for you, man." Brayden's voice interrupted his thoughts, and Micah tuned back in to what his friend was saying.

"Thanks," Micah said. "Let me know if you need help with the filmmaker."

A sour look crossed Brayden's face. "I can handle her."

"I know you can. But I'm here if you need me."

He walked back to his desk and logged off his computer. Time to visit Bea. Chunk rose from his bed, clearly aware of the time, as well.

"Ready to go, buddy?"

The drive passed in a blur. Micah was so focused on seeing her again, he barely noticed his surroundings. He helped Chunk from the backseat and practically ran to her door. Anticipation and excitement thrummed in his veins, making him almost giddy.

She opened the door before he could ring the bell, greeting them both with a smile. "I was getting worried."

"Sorry," he said, reaching for her. "We had a meeting. Ran a bit late."

She tilted her face up for his kiss. "No worries. I'm just glad you're here now."

She closed the door behind them, and when she turned back to face him, Micah was struck by a wave of love so powerful it nearly brought him to his knees.

Now. It has to be now.

He fumbled in his pocket and dropped to his knees. Bea's eyes widened as he took her hands.

"I meant to make this special for you, but I can't wait another minute." His stomach danced with nerves, his heart pounding in his chest.

"Micah?" She whispered his name, a hopeful question that made him nod.

"I love you. I never stopped loving you. And I know I never will. I want to be with you for the rest of my life. Will you marry me?"

He held up the ring and she clapped her hand over her mouth. Her eyes darted from it to his face. "Oh!" Tears welled in her eyes and she knelt before him, then threw her arms around his neck.

"I take it that's a yes?"

She pulled back and kissed him soundly. "Yes!" Another kiss, and then another. "Of course it's a yes!" She leaned forward to kiss him again, but Chunk's tongue swiped their cheeks before their lips met. They both turned to look at the dog who was sitting right next to them, tail thumping madly.

"I suppose you can be the ring bearer," Bea said with a laugh, reaching out to scratch behind the dog's ears.

Chunk closed his eyes and sighed, apparently accepting his new role.

Micah took Bea's left hand and slipped the ring onto her finger. She stared at it for a moment, turning her hand this way and that so the green stone sparkled in the light.

"It was my mom's," he said. "My aunt took it after she died, probably because she knew my dad would pawn it for booze money. She left it to me, along with the house."

"It's beautiful."

"I know it's not a diamond," he said, feeling suddenly shy. "I can get you one if you want. But I wanted you to have this first."

"I love it." She cupped his face in her hands. "The emerald matches your eyes."

"Think so?"

"Yes." She smiled, but then a shadow crossed her face.

"What's wrong?"

"Please don't take this the wrong way, but…" She trailed off and his stomach twisted with worry.

"What is it?"

"The Groom Killer," she said, gripping his shoulder. "Should we keep this quiet until after you solve the case? I wouldn't be able to handle it if you were a target because we'd gotten engaged."

The tension drained from his body along with his breath, and he felt almost light-headed with relief. "We can do that, if it makes you feel better."

Bea nodded. "It does. Believe me, I want to shout from the rooftops that we're engaged, but I don't want to risk your safety." She slipped his ring off her finger and transferred it to her right hand. "Are you sure you're okay with that?"

Micah smiled. "If it makes you feel better, I'm fine with it. But I can take care of myself, you know."

Bea kissed him gently, her fingers tangling in his hair. "I know. But we're partners now. And partners take care of each other."

Micah drew her against his chest, feeling whole for the first time in years. "I like the sound of that."

Bea laughed, her body vibrating against his. "I'm glad to hear it. Because I'm going to keep saying it for the rest of our lives."

"Promise?"

"I do."

* * * * *

LET'S TALK
Romance

For exclusive extracts, competitions
and special offers, find us online:

f facebook.com/millsandboon

◎ @millsandboonuk

🐦 @millsandboon

Or get in touch on 0844 844 1351*

For all the latest titles coming soon, visit
millsandboon.co.uk/nextmonth